Don Quixote
唐吉訶德

Original Author   Miguel de Cervantes Saavedra
Adaptor   Michael Robert Bradie
Illustrator   Nika Tchaikovskaya

WORDS
800

MP3

Let's Enjoy Masterpieces!

All the beautiful fairy tales and masterpieces that you have encountered during your childhood remain as warm memories in your adulthood. This time, let's indulge in the world of masterpieces through English. You can enjoy the depth and beauty of original works, which you can't enjoy through Chinese translations.

The stories are easy for you to understand because of your familiarity with them. When you enjoy reading, your ability to understand English will also rapidly improve.

This series of *Let's Enjoy Masterpieces* is a special reading comprehension booster program, devised to improve reading comprehension for beginners whose command of English is not satisfactory, or who are elementary, middle, and high school students. With this program, you can enjoy reading masterpieces in English with fun and efficiency.

This carefully planned program is composed of 5 levels, from the beginner level of 350 words to the intermediate and advanced levels of 1,000 words. With this program's level-by-level system, you are able to read famous texts in English and to savor the true pleasure of the world's language.

The program is well conceived, composed of reader-friendly explanations of English expressions and grammar, quizzes to help the student learn vocabulary and understand the meaning of the texts, and fabulous illustrations that adorn every page. In addition, with our "Guide to Listening," not only is reading comprehension enhanced but also listening comprehension skills are highlighted.

In the audio recording of the book, texts are vividly read by professional American actors. The texts are rewritten, according to the levels of the readers by an expert editorial staff of native speakers, on the basis of standard American English with the ministry of education recommended vocabulary. Therefore, it will be of great help even for all the students that want to learn English.

Please indulge yourself in the fun of reading and listening to English through *Let's Enjoy Masterpieces*.

米格爾 · 德 · 塞萬提斯

Miguel de Cervantes Saavedra
(1547–1616)

Miguel de Cervantes, a Spanish poet, novelist, and playwright, was born in Alcala de Henares near Madrid as the fourth child of a poor family. He couldn't have a proper education at school.

He went to Italy in 1569, where he was in the service of a cardinal, and the following year he enlisted in the army and stayed in the service for 5 years. While returning to Spain in 1575, he was captured by Barbary pirates and was sold as a slave. He eventually became the property of the viceroy of Algiers. Although in 1580 he was ransomed by his parents and the Trinitarians and returned to his family in Spain, his life was less than successful. He had a hard time working as a writer, a purchasing agent, and a tax collector. He was imprisoned twice for irregularities in his accounts.

Finally, in 1605 he had a huge success with the first volume of his great work Don Quixote. The book did not make him rich, but it brought him a great reputation as a man of letters. Afterward he published lots of novels and plays, and in 1615 he published the 2nd volume of Don Quixote.

Despite his success in writing, he never had enough money to live a comfortable life. He died in Madrid on April 23, 1616, at the age of 69, one year after the publication the 2nd volume of *Don Quixote*. Despite his many difficulties, Miguel de Cervantes Saavedra maintained a positive attitude and good mental health until he died.

Don Quixote

Don Quixote's fully title is *The Ingenious Hidalgo Don Quixote of La Mancha*. This novel is one of the classics and ranks high on the lists of the greatest works of fiction ever published. It has given unique inspirations to various literary genres. Don Quixote and his servant Sancho, two main characters in the book with their conflicting attitudes and personalities, have been much loved regardless of ages and nations.

Alonso Quixano, who is in his fifties and lives in La Mancha, Spain, is so obsessed with stories about brave errant knights that he is in a senile and confused state. He believes himself to be a knight called "Don Quixote" and sets out to receive the title of knight with his old skinny horse named "Rocinante."

After Don Quixote has been disgraced and beaten up by a trader from Toledo, he goes back home. Then Don Quixote successfully persuades his servant Sancho Panza to accompany him on a new adventure. The two sneak off in the early morning. From then on, their ridiculous adventure moves forward and is full of comedy and humor . . .

HOW TO USE THIS BOOK
本書使用說明

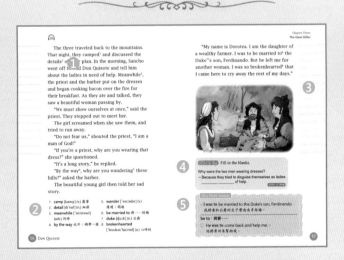

1 Original English texts

It is easy to understand the meaning of the text, because the text is rewritten according to the levels of the readers.

2 Explanation of the vocabulary

The words and expressions that include vocabulary above the elementary level are clearly defined.

3 Response notes

Spaces are included in the book so you can take notes about what you don't understand or what you want to remember.

4 Check Up

Review quizzes to check your understanding of the text.

5 One Point Lesson

In-depth analyses of major grammar points and expressions help you to understand sentences with difficult grammar.

🎧 Audio Recording

In the audio recording, native speakers narrate the texts in standard American English. By combining the written words and the audio recording, you can listen to English with great ease.

Audio books have been popular in Britain and America for many decades. They allow the listener to experience the proper word pronunciation and sentence intonation that add important meaning and drama to spoken English. Students will benefit from listening to the recording twenty or more times.

After you are familiar with the text and recording, listen once more with your eyes closed to check your listening comprehension. Finally, after you can listen with your eyes closed and understand every word and every sentence, you are then ready to mimic the native speaker.

Then you should make a recording by reading the text yourself. Then play both recordings to compare your oral skills with those of a native speaker.

HOW TO IMPROVE READING ABILITY

如何增進英文閱讀能力

① *Catch key words*

Read the key words in the sentences and practice catching the gist of the meaning of the sentence. You might question how working with a few important words could enhance your reading ability. However, it's quite effective. If you continue to use this method, you will find out that the key words and your knowledge of people and situations enables you to understand the sentence.

② *Divide long sentences*

Read in chunks of meaning, dividing sentences into meaningful chunks of information. In the book, chunks are arranged in sentences according to meaning. If you consider the sentences backwards or grammatically, your reading speed will be slow and you will find it difficult to listen to English.

You are ready to move to a more sophisticated level of comprehension when you find that narrowly focusing on chunks is irritating. Instead of considering the chunks, you will make it a habit to read the sentence from the beginning to the end to figure out the meaning of the whole.

③ *Make inferences and assumptions*

Making inferences and assumptions is part of your ability. If you don't know, try to guess the meaning of the words. Although you don't know all the words in context, don't go straight to the dictionary. Developing an ability to make inferences in the context is important.

The first way to figure out the meaning of a word is from its context. If you cannot make head or tail out of the meaning of a word, look at what comes before or after it. Ask yourself what can happen in such a situation. Make your best guess as to the word's meaning. Then check the explanations of the word in the book or look up the word in a dictionary.

④ *Read a lot and reread the same book many times*

There is no shortcut to mastering English. Only if you do a lot of reading will you make your way to the summit. Read fun and easy books with an average of less than one new word per page. Try to immerse yourself in English as often as you can.

Spend time "swimming" in English. Language learning research has shown that immersing yourself in English will help you improve your English, even though you may not be aware of what you're learning.

CONTENTS

Before You Read

Don Quixote

I was born Alonso Quixano, but have given myself the name Don Quixote. I was also known as the Knight of the Long Face, so named by my squire[1], during our difficult adventures[2]. However, every great knight has difficulties[3]. He should never quit because that would be shameful[4].

Sancho Panza

I was a farmer before I became my master's squire. He promised me that our adventures would make me rich. However, I am beginning to think my master is not quite sane[5]. He attacks[6] sheep and windmills. I try to tell him that they are only sheep and windmills, but he thinks they are enemy[7] armies and evil[8] giants[9].

1. **squire** [skwaɪr] (n.) 扈從
2. **adventure** [ədˋventʃər] (n.) 冒險
3. **difficulty** [ˋdɪfɪkəltɪ] (n.) 困難
4. **shameful** [ˋʃeɪmfəl] (a.) 可恥的；丟臉的
5. **sane** [seɪn] (a.) 神智正常的
6. **attack** [əˋtæk] (v.) 攻擊
7. **enemy** [ˋenəmɪ] (a.) 敵人的
8. **evil** [ˋiːvəl] (a.) 邪惡的；罪惡的
9. **giant** [ˋdʒaɪənt] (n.) 巨人

Priest and Barber

We are friends of Don Quixote. We are getting very worried about him. He used to[10] be just an ordinary[11] landowner[12]. Then he went crazy, reading adventure stories. We must do something to make him wake up to reality[13]!

Carrasco

Don Quixote's friends convinced[14] me to try to get Don Quixote to stay home. Perhaps if I pretended[15] to be a knight and challenged Don Quixote to a duel[16], I could get him to promise to stay home if he loses.

Dutch and Duchess

We just love Don Quixote. He was so funny! We gave him a great feast[17] in our castle and delighted[18] to hear his crazy stories. We also had Don Quixote and his servant ride a fake[19] horse in our courtyard blindfolded[20]. It was so funny!

10. **used to** 曾經
11. **ordinary** [ˋɔːrdəneri] (a.) 平常的；普通的
12. **landowner** [ˋlændˌoʊnər] (n.) 地主
13. **reality** [rɪˋælɪti] (n.) 真實；事實
14. **convince A to** 說服某人去……
15. **pretend** [prɪˋtend] (v.) 假裝

16. **duel** [ˋduːəl] (n.) 決鬥
17. **feast** [fiːst] (n.) 筵席
18. **delighted** [dɪˋlaɪtɪd] (a.) 高興的；愉悅的
19. **fake** [feɪk] (a.) 假的；冒充的
20. **blindfolded** [ˋblaɪndfoʊldɪd] (a.) 蒙住眼睛的

13

Chapter One

🎧1 A Gentleman from La Mancha

In the Spanish village of La Mancha, there lived a gentleman who loved to read. His favorite stories were of knights[1] and their code[2] of chivalry[3]: full of dragons[4], magic[5] swords[6], enchanted[7] forests, and damsels[8] in distress[9].

This gentleman was not a wealthy man, but rather a hidalgo[10]. A hidalgo was a landowner[11] who was richer than a peasant[12], but poorer than a nobleman[13]. His name was Senor[14] Quixano.

1. **knight** [naɪt] (n.) 騎士
2. **code** [koʊd] (n.) 行為規範
3. **chivalry** [ˈʃɪvəlri] (n.) 騎士精神
4. **dragon** [ˈdrægən] (n.) 龍
5. **magic** [ˈmædʒɪk] (a.) 魔法的
6. **sword** [sɔːrd] (n.) 劍
7. **enchanted** [ɪnˈtʃæntɪd] (a.) 施過魔法的
8. **damsel** [ˈdæmzəl] (n.) 少女
9. **in distress** 遇難
10. **hidalgo** [hɪˈdælgoʊ] (n.) 西班牙紳士
11. **landowner** [ˈlændˌoʊnər] (n.) 地主
12. **peasant** [ˈpezənt] (n.) 農夫
13. **nobleman** [ˈnoʊbəlmən] (n.) 貴族
14. **senor** [seɪnˈjɔːr] (n.) 先生；紳士
15. **modestly** [ˈmɑːdɪstli] (adv.) 謙虛地

Senor Quixano lived modestly[15] with his housekeeper[16] and his young niece[17]. He was a tall, thin man in his fifties. He was a strong and healthy man, who went hunting every morning.

However, he started to read adventure[18] stories all the time. His best friends, the local priest[19] and the village barber[20], were worried. Their friend suddenly began spending night and day in his chair, reading adventure books through crazed[21], bloodshot[22] eyes.

Soon he started thinking these stories were true. Finally he went completely crazy.

16. **housekeeper** [ˋhaʊsˌkiːpər] (n.) 管家
17. **niece** [niːs] (n.) 姪女；外甥女
18. **adventure** [ədˋventʃər] (n.) 冒險
19. **priest** [priːst] (n.) 牧師
20. **barber** [ˋbɑːrbər] (n.) 理髮師
21. **crazed** [ˋkreɪzd] (a.) 瘋狂的
22. **bloodshot** [ˋblʌdʃɑːt] (a.) 布滿血絲的

Waking up in his reading chair one morning, Senor Quixano announced[1], "I'm going to become a knight-errant[2]!"

"A what?" asked his concerned[3] niece.

"A knight-errant is a righter[4] of wrongs, a friend to the unfortunate, a rescuer[5] of fair[6] maidens[7], and a killer of dragons!"

1. **announce** [əˋnaʊns] (v.)
   宣布；聲稱
2. **knight-errant** [ˏnaɪtˋerənt]
   (n.) 遊俠騎士
3. **concerned** [kənˋsɜːrnd] (a.)
   憂心的
4. **righter** [ˋraɪtər] (n.) 改正者
5. **rescuer** [ˋrɛskjuːər] (n.)
   援助者
6. **fair** [fer] (a.) 美麗的
7. **maiden** [ˋmeɪdən] (n.) 少女
8. **attic** [ˋætɪk] (n.) 頂樓；閣樓
9. **rusty** [ˋrʌsti] (a.) 生鏽的
10. **armor** [ˋɑːrmər] (n.) 盔甲
11. **bold** [boʊld] (a.)
    大膽的；英勇的
12. **faithful** [ˋfeɪθfəl] (v.) 忠實的
13. **steed** [stiːd] (n.) 坐騎

"But Uncle," she cried, "there are no dragons in Spain! And who are these maidens who need rescuing?"

The old man went to the attic[8] of his house and found a rusty[9] old suit of armor[10]. He put the suit on and felt ready for action.

In a bold[11] voice, he announced, "Now, to my faithful[12] steed[13]!"

This "steed" was really a worn-out[14] nag[15]. But to his delusional[16] eyes, it was a valiant[17] war horse.

"I name you Rocinante, Queen of the hacks[18]! And I will call myself. . ."

He took a moment to think of the perfect name. "Don Quixote!"

This is the Spanish equivalent[19] of Sir Thigh[20]-piece.

✓Check Up Fill in the blanks.

Senor Quixano named himself _____, and his horse _____.

Ans: Don Quixote, Rocinante

---

14. **worn-out** [ˋwɔːrnaʊt] (a.) 過時的

15. **nag** [næg] (n.) 老馬

16. **delusional** [dɪˋluʒənəl] (a.) 妄想的

17. **valiant** [ˋvæliənt] (a.) 英勇的

18. **hack** [hæk] (n.) 老馬

19. **equivalent** [ɪˋkwɪvələnt] (n.) 相等物；同義字

20. **thigh** [θaɪ] (n.) 大腿

"Now I must dedicate my life to[1] a lady!"

"Do you know a lady?" sobbed[2] the man's niece, frightened[3] by his insane[4] ramblings[5].

"All knights know a lady," the man replied. "When I conquer[6] a giant or capture[7] a villain[8], I'll parade[9] them in front of her to prove my love and loyalty[10]."

Then he remembered stories he had heard of a beautiful peasant girl[11] from the nearby village of El Toboso. Having lost his grip on[12] reality, he decided that she was a lonely princess.

"What's her name?" demanded[13] his niece, hoping to bring him to his senses[14].

Quickly, he invented a name. "All of the sweetest ladies are named Dulcinea. Her name is Dulcinea del Toboso, and to her I dedicate my life! Don't try to stop me. I must go!"

1. **dedicate *A* to *B***
   將 A 奉獻給 B
2. **sob** [sɑːb] (v.) 哭訴；嗚咽
3. **frighten** [ˋfraɪtn] (v.)
   使害怕；使受驚
4. **insane** [ɪnˋseɪn] (a.) 瘋狂的
5. **rambling** [ˋræmblɪŋ] (n.)
   雜亂無章的話
6. **conquer** [ˋkɑːŋkər] (v.)
   征服
7. **capture** [ˋkæptʃər] (v.) 捕獲
8. **villain** [ˋvɪlən] (n.)
   壞人；惡棍
9. **parade** [pəˋreɪd] (v.) 炫耀
10. **loyalty** [ˋlɔɪəlti] (n.)
    忠誠；忠心
11. **peasant girl** 鄉下姑娘
12. **grip on** 抓住
13. **demand** [dɪˋmænd] (v.) 查問

Then he picked up his sword, a cracked[15] old lance[16], and a leather[17] shield[18] and marched[19] out to the stable[20]. A few minutes later, he rode out in search of his first knightly[21] adventure.

Don Quixote soon realized that he had not been knighted. "I must find a lord or lady to dub[22] me a knight," he said. "I don't want to be called a fraud[23]!"

14. **bring** *A* **to one's senses** 使⋯⋯甦醒
15. **cracked** [krækt] (a.) 破裂的
16. **lance** [læns] (n.) 長矛
17. **leather** [ˋlɛðər] (a.) 皮製的
18. **shield** [ʃiːld] (n.) 盾；防護物
19. **march** [mɑːrtʃ] (v.) 前進
20. **stable** [ˋsteɪbəl] (n.) 馬廄
21. **knightly** [ˋnaɪtli] (a.) 騎士的
22. **dub** [dʌb] (v.) 將⋯⋯冠以⋯⋯；授予⋯⋯封號
23. **fraud** [frɔːd] (n.) 騙子

🎧 4

All day Don Quixote rode the scorching[1] plain[2] searching for adventure, but nothing happened. By sunset, he and Rocinante were hungry and tired. In the fading[3] light, the armored[4] man saw an inn[5] and rode toward it. "Perhaps we'll find shelter[6] at that castle," he said to his horse.

1. **scorching** [`skɔːrtʃɪŋ] (a.) 酷熱的
2. **plain** [pleɪn] (n.) 草原
3. **fading** [`feɪdɪŋ] (a.) 逐漸消失的
4. **armored** [`ɑːrmərd] (a.) 裝甲的
5. **inn** [ɪn] (n.) 小旅館
6. **shelter** [`ʃeltər] (n.) 遮蓋物；避難所
7. **shabby** [`ʃæbi] (a.) 破爛的
8. **in shock** 處於震驚中
9. **approach** [ə`proʊtʃ] (v.) 接近
10. **summon** [`sʌmən] (v.) 召喚

The inn was of the common shabby[7] type found along the highways of Spain. In front of the inn were two dirty-faced peasant girls, who watched in shock[8] as this man in rusty armor approached[9] them.

"Good evening, fair maidens," he said. "I am the knight, Don Quixote de La Mancha. Please summon[10] a trumpeter to announce my arrival."

In his eyes, this old inn was a great castle with tall silver towers. Don Quixote became annoyed[11] when the girls just giggled[12].

But at this moment, a pig-handler stepped out of[13] the inn and blew[14] his horn[15] to round up[16] his grunting[17] animals for the night. Don Quixote mistook the sound of the horn for[18] a chorus of pipes and trumpets.

✓Check Up Fill in the blanks.

Don Quixote mistook the inn for a _____.

Ans: castle

11. **annoyed** [əˋnɔɪd] (a.) 惱怒的
12. **giggle** [ˋgɪgəl] (v.) 咯咯地笑
13. **step out of** 走出……
14. **blow** [bloʊ] (v.) 吹;吹奏

15. **horn** [hɔːrn] (n.) 號角;喇叭
16. **round up** 聚集;聚攏
17. **grunting** [ˋgrʌntɪŋ] (a.) 呼嚕叫的
18. **mistake *A* for *B*** 將 A 誤認為 B

Then the innkeeper[1] came to the knight. "If you're looking for a bed for the night, I'm sorry to tell you that we're all full."

"Sire[2], are you the master of this castle?" asked Don Quixote politely[3].

Looking at this man in his rusty armor, the innkeeper realized that he was obviously[4] crazy. The innkeeper decided to have some fun with this loon[5].

"All of the royal[6] apartments in my castle are full."

"That's okay," replied Don Quixote. "A good knight has no need for comfort[7]. I'll be happy to sleep on the ground with a rock for a pillow."

"You're a knight, aren't you?" the innkeeper asked mischievously[8].

"I am an apprentice[9] knight," replied Don Quixote. "I seek a kind lord who will dub me a knight with his sword."

1. **innkeeper** [ˋɪn͵kiːpər] (n.) 客棧老闆
2. **sire** [saɪr] (n.) 陛下
3. **politely** [pəˋlaɪtli] (adv.) 有禮貌地
4. **obviously** [ˋɑːbvɪəsli] (adv.) 明顯地
5. **loon** [luːn] (n.) 怪人
6. **royal** [ˋrɔɪəl] (a.) 王室的；盛大的

"I see," said the innkeeper, "but I'm busy now caring for[10] my other guests. I'll be back to you when I get a chance."

"Thank you, my lord," replied Don Quixote.

✓*Check Up* True or False.

T F 1. Don Quixote is looking for a lord who will make him a knight.

T F 2. The innkeeper is playing a joke on Don Quixote.

Ans: 1. T 2. T

7. **comfort** [`kʌmfərt] (n.)
   舒適；安慰

8. **mischievously** [`mɪstʃɪvəsli]
   (adv.) 淘氣地

9. **apprentice** [ə`prentɪs] (n.)
   學徒

10. **care for** 照料

After some rest, Don Quixote grew impatient and sent for[1] the innkeeper. When the innkeeper stumbled[2] out, Don Quixote said, "Lord, I can wait no longer. Please tell me what good deed[3] I must do to earn my knighthood[4]."

The innkeeper said, "If you want me to knight you, stay here and guard[5] my courtyard[6] tonight."

With that, he turned and stomped[7] off to the kitchen.

Don Quixote picked up his weapons and walked to the middle of the courtyard, next to a water trough[8]. Inside, the innkeeper told his guests about the madman who thought he was a knight in the courtyard.

A few hours later, a muleteer[9] approached the trough with his animals.

"Stand back, foolish knight!" shouted Don Quixote. "I will defend[10] this magic well to the death[11]!"

---

1. **send for** 派人去叫
2. **stumble** [ˋstʌmbəl] (v.) 絆腳;絆倒
3. **deed** [diːd] (n.) 行為
4. **knighthood** [ˋnaɪthʊd] (n.) 騎士稱號;騎士頭銜

5. **guard** [gɑːrd] (v.) 守衛
6. **courtyard** [ˋkɔːrtjɑːrd] (n.) 庭院
7. **stomp** [stɑːmp] (v.) 踩腳;重踩
8. **trough** [trɑːf] (n.) 飲水槽

"But my mules need water," cried the peasant as he pushed past Don Quixote.

Swinging[12] his lance, Don Quixote hit the man on the head and knocked him out[13].

"I have done my first good deed!" exclaimed[14] Don Quixote. "When this man awakes, I must send him to my lady Dulcinea to pay his respects."

9. **muleteer** [ˌmjuːlə`tɪər] (n.)
  趕騾的人
10. **defend** [dɪ`fɛnd] (v.)
  防禦；保衛
11. **to the death** 至死；到永遠

12. **swing** [swɪŋ] (v.)
  擺動；轉身
13. **knock out *A*** 使某人昏過去
14. **exclaim** [ɪk`skleɪm] (v.)
  呼喊；驚叫

Alarmed by the noise, the other muleteers rushed out of the inn and attacked Don Quixote.

"A swarm[1] of evil knights attacks me!" cried Don Quixote as he blocked[2] their flying stones with his shield.

The innkeeper realized that he needed to get rid of[3] this dangerous screwball[4].

1. **swarm** [swɔːrm] (n.) 群；許多
2. **block** [blɑːk] (v.) 阻擋
3. **get rid of** 擺脫；丟掉
4. **screwball** [ˋskruːbɔːl] (n.) 怪人；狂人
5. **forgive** [fərˋgɪv] (v.) 原諒
6. **put down** 放下
7. **courage** [ˋkɜːrɪdʒ] (n.) 勇氣
8. **kneel down** 單膝跪地
9. **obediently** [ouˋbidiəntli] (adv.) 服從地

"Dear knight," he said to Don Quixote, "forgive[5] these evil knights and put down[6] your weapons. You have proved your courage[7]. I will dub you a knight without delay. Kneel down[8]."

Obediently[9], Don Quixote knelt amid the straw[10] and dung[11] of the yard.

"I hereby[12] appoint you to the order of righteous[13] knights," cried the innkeeper, smacking[14] Don Quixote across the back with his own sword.

Don Quixote jumped to his feet[15] excitedly, "My lord, I owe you everything!"

"Yes, yes," replied the innkeeper. "Now you must go off[16] on your good-deed doing and wrong-righting."

"At once[17]!" cried Don Quixote, who hurried to the stable, mounted[18] Rocinante, and rode out into the dawn[19] of La Mancha.

10. **straw** [strɔː] (n.) 稻草；吸管
11. **dung** [dʌŋ] (n.) 糞肥
12. **hereby** [ˌhɪrˋbaɪ] (adv.) 藉此
13. **righteous** [ˋraɪtʃəs] (a.) 公正的；正直的
14. **smack** [smæk] (v.) 打；摑
15. **jump to one's feet** 一躍而起
16. **go off** 動身；離去
17. **at once** 馬上
18. **mount** [maʊnt] (v.) 騎上
19. **dawn** [dɔːn] (n.) 黎明

Shortly after, Don Quixote spotted[1] a group of silk merchants coming toward him on the road.

"Here is an opportunity[2] for gallantry[3]."

Riding in front of the group, he blocked the road. "Halt[4], cretins[5]! None shall be allowed to pass without proclaiming[6] that my lady, Dulcinea del Toboso, is the most beautiful maiden in the world!"

The traders[7] stopped and looked at each other. It was obvious to them that they were in the presence of[8] a madman.

"I want to see her first before I can proclaim her beauty. How do we know that she's not just some old sloppy chops[9]?" said the joker[10] of the group.

"Sloppy chops?" screamed[11] Don Quixote. "Prepare to do battle[12], you impudent[13] knave[14]!" Don Quixote raised his lance and charged[15] the group. But Rocinante was not accustomed to[16] speed and stumbled. Don Quixote was thrown through the air and landed in a ditch[17] with a crash. The merchants went away, laughing loudly.

---

1. **spot** [spɑːt] (v.) 看見；發現
2. **opportunity** [ˌɑːpərˋtuːnəti] (n.) 機會；良機
3. **gallantry** [ˋgæləntri] (n.) 英勇行為
4. **halt** [hɔːlt] (v.) 停止；終止
5. **cretin** [ˋkriːtn] (n.) 笨蛋；傻瓜

Hours later, a passing farmer heard a whimper[18]. He found Don Quixote in the ditch, covered in mud. The farmer recognized him as Senor Quixano from the village. He hurriedly picked up Don Quixote and carried him home. There the knight was tucked safely into[19] his own bed.

6. **proclaim** [proʊˋklem] (v.) 宣布；聲明

7. **trader** [ˋtreɪdər] (n.) 商人

8. **in the presence of** 在……的面前

9. **sloppy chop** 又老又肥的女人

10. **joker** [ˋdʒoʊkər] (n.) 愛開玩笑的人

11. **scream** [skriːm] (v.) 尖叫

12. **do battle** 作戰

13. **impudent** [ˋɪmpjʊdənt] (a.) 粗魯的

14. **knave** [neɪv] (n.) 無賴；惡棍

15. **charge** [tʃɑːrdʒ] (v.) 進攻

16. **be accustomed to** 習慣於

17. **ditch** [dɪtʃ] (n.) 溝；渠

18. **whimper** [ˋwɪmpər] (n.) 啜泣

19. **tuck into** 抱膝入……

A Match.

❶ Don Quixote •

❷ The innkeeper •

❸ Senor Quixano's • niece

❹ The joker •

• ⓐ But Uncle, there are no dragons in Spain!

• ⓑ But how do we know that she's not just some old sloppy chops?

• ⓒ I don't want to be called a fraud!

• ⓓ All of the royal apartments in my castle are full.

B Fill in the blanks with given words.

chivalry   battle   hidalgo   dub

❶ His favorite stories were of knights and their code of _____.

❷ A _____ was a landowner who was richer than a peasant but poorer than a nobleman.

❸ I seek a kind lord who will _____ me a knight.

❹ Prepare to do _____, you impudent knave.

C Choose the correct answer.

❶ Why were Senor Quixano's friends and family worried about him?

(a) Because he stopped waking up early in the morning.

(b) Because he began reading adventure stories all the time and thought they were real.

(c) Because he had dark skin from years under the harsh Spanish sun.

❷ What did Don Quixote want the silk merchants to do?

(a) He wanted them to proclaim the beauty of his lady, Dulcinea del Toboso.

(b) He wanted them to give him all of their money.

(c) He wanted them to dub him a knight.

D True or False.

T F ❶ Senor Quixano was a very wealthy peasant.

T F ❷ Senor Quixano's niece was worried when he decided to become a knight.

T F ❸ The innkeeper thought Don Quixote was crazy.

T F ❹ Don Quixote became a friend of the muleteers.

T F ❺ Rocinante was not accustomed to speed.

· Chapter Two ·

🎧9 Knight & Squire[1]

For two weeks Don Quixote rested in his house, making everyone think he had regained[2] his sanity[3]. But he had secretly sold some of his land to finance[4] his next adventure. He was also looking for a squire to accompany[5] him.

The only man Don Quixote found who would work for him was a fat little farmer named Sancho Panza. He was a total dunce[6].

"This squire job sounds like hard work," said Sancho. "I'd rather be at home with my family, munching[7] on a big plate of[8] pork."

1. **squire** [skwaɪr] (n.) 扈從
2. **regain** [rɪˋgeɪn] (v.) 恢復
3. **sanity** [ˋsænɪtɪ] (n.) 神智正常
4. **finance** [ˋfaɪnæns] (v.) 為……籌資金
5. **accompany** [əˋkʌmpənɪ] (v.) 陪伴；伴隨
6. **dunce** [dʌns] (n.) 愚笨的人
7. **munch** [mʌntʃ] (v.) 大聲咀嚼

8. **a plate of** 一盤
9. **nap** [næp] (n.) 打盹兒；午睡
10. **serve** [sɜːrv] (v.) 服務；服侍
11. **end up** 最終成為
12. **governor** [ˋgʌvənər] (n.) 總督；州長
13. **lick** [lɪk] (v.) 舔；舐
14. **grab** [græb] (v.) 攫取；抓取
15. **saddle** [ˋsædel] (v.) 套上馬鞍
16. **donkey** [ˋdɑːŋkɪ] (n.) 驢

Sancho Panza loved wine, food, and afternoon naps[9] more than anything else.

"But squires always receive great prizes of gold and land from the knights they serve[10]," promised Don Quixote. "If you serve me, you'll surely end up[11] as the governor[12] of some rich island."

"My own island!" Sancho repeated, licking[13] his lips. "Okay, I'll grab[14] my bags and saddle[15] up my donkey[16]."

Then the two left in the middle of the night without telling anyone.

✓Check Up Fill in the blanks.

Sancho was hired as Don Quixote's _____.

Ans: squire

By dawn, the two men were in the middle of a wide plain. Squinting[1] in the glare[2] of the brilliant[3] sun, Don Quixote saw thirty or forty windmills[4] in the fields before them.

"Sancho, fortune is smiling upon us!" he called.

"Does that mean it's time for breakfast?" replied Sancho.

"This is no time for eating, you pig. Look at those giants over there. I'll kill every one of them. Our great service will be remembered for centuries[5]!"

"What giants?" cried Sancho Panza.

"Over there! The ones with the long arms!"

"But Master, those are windmills."

"Don't contradict[6] me," scolded[7] Don Quixote. "I know an army of[8] giants when I see them!"

Don Quixote spurred[9] Rocinante into a gallop[10] and raised his lance.

"Giants! Prepare to fight!" he shouted.

Charging into the nearest tower, he thrust[11] the shaft[12] of his lance into a sweeping sail[13]. The weapon shattered[14], and the knight was picked up off his horse and tossed[15] into the air.

He landed with a great "BOOM[16]!" fifty meters away in a large puff[17] of white dust[18].

✓*Check Up* Fill in the blanks.

Don Quixote thought the windmills and their sails were _____ and their _____.

Ans: giants, arms

---

1. **squint** [skwɪnt] (v.) 斜眼看
2. **glare** [glɛr] (n.) 刺眼的強光
3. **brilliant** [`brɪljənt] (a.) 明亮的
4. **windmill** [`wɪndˌmɪl] (n.) 風車
5. **century** [`sɛntʃəri] (n.) 世紀
6. **contradict** [ˌkɑːntrə`dɪkt] (v.) 反駁
7. **scold** [skoʊld] (v.) 責罵
8. **an army of** 一群
9. **spur** [spɜːr] (v.) 策馬飛奔
10. **gallop** [`gæləp] (n.) 疾馳
11. **thrust** [θrʌst] (v.) 刺
12. **shaft** [ʃæft] (n.) 矛柄
13. **sail** [`seɪl] (n.) 風車（翼板）
14. **shatter** [`ʃætər] (v.) 粉碎
15. **toss** [tɔːs] (v.) 拋；投
16. **boom** [buːm] (n.) 隆隆聲
17. **puff** [pʌf] (n.) 一陣；一股
18. **dust** [dʌst] (n.) 灰塵

Trotting[1] over on his donkey, Sancho Panza said, "I told you they were windmills."

"You fool!" said Don Quixote. "When I charged those giants, an evil wizard flew by on an invisible[2] horse and cast a spell that changed them into windmills! To rob me of[3] my glory!"

"I see," said Sancho, believing every word as he helped his master to his feet[4].

"Don't worry, my squire. I'll find this wizard and destroy him!"

The next morning, they began traveling again without breakfast, to Sancho's dismay[5]. An hour later, they saw a large cloud of dust in the distance[6].

"It must be two bloodthirsty[7] armies in battle!" exclaimed Don Quixote. Then he quickly described[8] both of the armies, including the names of their generals[9] and fiercest[10] knights which he made up.

1. **trot** [trɑːt] (v.) 策馬小跑
2. **invisible** [ɪnˋvɪzɪbəl] (a.) 隱形的
3. **rob A of B** 從 A 身上盜取 B
4. **to one's feet** 站起來
5. **to one's dismay** 令某人感到沮喪
6. **in the distance** 在遠處
7. **bloodthirsty** [ˋblʌdˏθɜːrsti] (a.) 嗜殺成性的
8. **describe** [dɪˋskraɪb] (v.) 描述

"How do we know that this isn't just a trick[11] by those evil wizards?"

"Can't you hear thousands of marching feet?" yelled Don Quixote, who raised his broken lance and charged them.

"They're not soldiers," cried Sancho, "It's just a large flock of[12] sheep!"

9. **general** [ˋdʒenərəl] (n.) 將軍
10. **fierce** [fɪrs] (a.) 兇猛的
11. **trick** [trɪk] (n.) 詭計；把戲
12. **a flock of** 一群

The knight began skewering[1] the poor sheep on the end of his lance. As soon as the shepherds[2] saw him killing their animals, they began pelting[3] him with stones. A rock smashed[4] the side of Don Quixote's face and knocked him off Rocinante.

"Those evil wizards!" cried Don Quixote, spitting out[5] a mouthful of blood and the chips[6] of broken teeth. "They've done it again!"

In a nearby meadow[7], the knight and the squire found a place to rest for the night.

"I'll have dinner ready in a minute," said Sancho.

"Oh, Squire, how can you think of eating in the moment of my greatest despair[8]?"

"There's nothing more important to me than eating," Sancho said devouring[9] raw[10] onion and salami[11]. "What are you so sad about anyway?"

Holding his throbbing[12] head, the knight answered, "The loss[13] of half my ear and four teeth saddens[14] me."

"I'm not surprised. There will be nothing left of you in a week or two. I've never seen a man more miserable[15]. We should call you the Knight of the Long Face[16]. Your chin is almost scraping[17] the ground."

"Yes, my squire, that's an excellent name for such an unhappy knight as myself."

1. **skewer** [ˋskjuːər] (v.) 用扦串起
2. **shepherd** [ˋʃepərd] (n.) 牧羊人
3. **pelt** [pelt] (v.) 投擲；開火
4. **smash** [smæʃ] (v.) 猛撞；猛擊
5. **spit out** 吐出
6. **chip** [tʃɪp] (n.) 屑片
7. **meadow** [ˋmedoʊ] (n.) 草地；牧草地
8. **despair** [dɪˋsper] (n.) 絕望
9. **devour** [dɪˋvaʊr] (v.) 狼吞虎嚥
10. **raw** [rɔː] (a.) 生的
11. **salami** [səˋlɑːmi] (n.) 薩拉米香腸
12. **throb** [θrɑːb] (v.) 陣陣作痛
13. **loss** [lɔːs] (n.) 喪失
14. **sadden** [ˋsædən] (v.) 使難過
15. **miserable** [ˋmɪzərəbəl] (a.) 痛苦的；悽慘的
16. **long face** 愁眉苦臉
17. **scrape** [skreɪp] (v.) 刮；擦

🎧 13

The two realized that they were thirsty. An hour later, they located[1] a stream[2] in the forest. As the sun began to set, they heard a terrible sound coming from within the depths of the forest.

"This is an enchanted forest ruled by a terrible ogre[3]. I will find and destroy him with my lightning[4] lance. If I'm not back in three days, go to my lady Dulcinea and tell her I died valiantly in her honor."

Sancho Panza was afraid to be left alone[5], so he slipped off[6] his donkey and sneaked[7] under Rocinante's hind legs[8]. There he tied a loop[9] of rope to hold her still.

When Don Quixote tried to spur the nag on, she could not move.

"What magic is this?" boomed Don Quixote. "My steed is held still."

"Oh, it must be that evil wizard again," lied Sancho. "Perhaps it would be better to destroy the ogre in the morning."

"Yes, I will break this spell in the morning," agreed Don Quixote.

Check Up Choose the correct answer.

Sancho held Rocinante still with rope because _____.
A the horse ran wild
B he did not want to be alone
C his master feared the evil wizard

Ans: B

1. **locate** [`loʊkeɪt] (v.) 發現……的位置
2. **stream** [striːm] (n.) 小河；溪流
3. **ogre** [`oʊgər] (n.) 食人惡魔
4. **lightning** [`laɪtnɪŋ] (a.) 雷電的
5. **be left alone** 被獨自留下
6. **slip off** 滑落
7. **sneak** [sniːk] (v.) 溜走
8. **hind legs** 後肢
9. **loop** [luːp] (n.) 圈

The two men spent the rest of the night trembling[1] in the forest for fear of the terrible noise coming from down the river.

At dawn, Sancho slipped[2] the rope from Rocinante's hind legs. When Don Quixote mounted her, she could walk.

"I'm free!" exclaimed the knight happily. Then they set off[3] to search for[4] the ogre.

But when they found the source[5] of the terrible crashing sound, it wasn't an ogre but an old water machine, clanking[6] away under the power of a waterfall[7].

1. **tremble** [ˋtrɛmbəl] (v.) 顫抖
2. **slip** [slɪp] (v.) 滑動
3. **set off** 出發
4. **search for** 尋找
5. **source** [sɔrs] (n.) 來源
6. **clank** [klæŋk] (v.) 發出噹啷聲
7. **waterfall** [ˋwɔtɚˏfɔl] (n.) 瀑布
8. **folly** [ˋfɑli] (n.) 愚蠢的想法
9. **in fear of** 害怕
10. **failed** [feɪld] (a.) 失敗的
11. **lift one's spirits** 提振士氣
12. **valuable** [ˋvæljʊbəl] (a.) 有價值的
13. **wash basin** 銅盆
14. **challenge** [ˋtʃælɪndʒ] (v.) 挑戰

Sancho Panza began laughing at Don Quixote's newest folly[8]. "We just spent the night trembling in fear of[9] this!" he laughed.

The Knight of the Long Face was even more miserable after this failed[10] adventure. But late that afternoon, he saw something that lifted his spirits[11].

"Look, Sancho, do you see that knight riding toward us?"

"I see a man on a donkey," replied Sancho.

"That knight is Horatio the Brave, and his helmet is the most valuable[12] on Earth."

"I think that's a barber's wash basin[13] on his head."

"No, it's a solid gold battle helmet. I will challenge[14] him and win it!"

Check Up Fill in the blanks.

Don Quixote thought _____ when his horse could walk.

A Rocinante got well

B the spell was broken

C the rope was released

Ans: B

🎧 15

Don Quixote shouted, "Surrender[1] your helmet, Horatio, or I'll spear[2] you with my lance!"

"I have no helmet," cried the man. "I'm just a barber. This brass basin is for my work. I put it on my head because it was raining."

"Do you expect me to believe that?" scoffed[3] Don Quixote, drawing[4] his sword.

Don Quixote snatched[5] the basin from the man and placed it on his head. "The visor[6] is missing, and someone has tried to melt[7] the gold off. But I shall wear it with pride."

Sancho tried not to giggle at the sight of Don Quixote with the wash basin on his head.

1. **surrender** [sə`rendər] (v.) 放棄
2. **spear** [spɪr] (v.) 用矛或魚叉刺
3. **scoff** [skɑːf] (v.) 譏諷
4. **draw** [drɔː] (v.) 拔出
5. **snatch** [snætʃ] (v.) 奪走
6. **visor** [`vaɪzər] (n.) 頭盔的面甲
7. **melt** [melt] (v.) 融化；熔化
8. **a dozen** 一打
9. **chain** [tʃeɪn] (n.) 鏈條
10. **herd** [hɜːrd] (v.) 把……綁在一起
11. **lash** [læʃ] (v.) 鞭打
12. **whip** [wɪp] (n.) 鞭子
13. **prisoner** [`prɪzənər] (n.) 囚犯
14. **row** [roʊ] (v.) 划船
15. **duty** [`duːti] (n.) 職責
16. **criminal** [`krɪmɪnəl] (n.) 罪犯

Later they came to a line of a dozen[8] men with heavy chains[9] around their necks and hands. Four soldiers herded[10] them, cursing and lashing[11] them with whips[12].

"Prisoners[13]," said Sancho, "off to row[14] the king's boat."

"I don't believe it," said Don Quixote. "These unfortunate men are being held against their will. It is my duty[15] to rescue them."

"Master," said Sancho with alarm, "these men are terrible criminals[16]. They must pay for their crimes!"

"Move aside!" commanded[1] one of the soldiers.

"These men are vulnerable[2] and needy[3]," said Don Quixote. "As a knight-errant, I offer[4] them protection[5]!"

"This crazy old fool is out of his mind[6]," laughed the sergeant. "He's got a wash basin on his head!"

As the other soldiers laughed, Don Quixote smashed the sergeant[7] over the head with his lance and knocked him unconscious[8]. The other soldiers attacked him, but the convicts[9] attacked them faster. One of the convicts stole the keys from the sergeant's pocket and unlocked the other criminals. The convicts overtook[10] the soldiers easily.

"My friends," cried Don Quixote, "I have given you freedom[11]. All I ask in return is that you go to the village of El Toboso and testify[12] of my courage to my mistress[13]."

"He's as crazy as a coconut!" yelled one of the convicts. "Grab him!"

1. **command** [kəˋmænd] (v.) 命令；指揮
2. **vulnerable** [ˋvʌlnərəbəl] (a.) 易受傷的
3. **needy** [ˋniːdi] (a.) 貧窮的
4. **offer** [ˋɑːfər] (v.) 提供
5. **protection** [prəˋtekʃən] (n.) 保護
6. **out of one's mind** 精神不正常
7. **sergeant** [ˋsɑːrdʒənt] (n.) 警官

The convicts attacked Don Quixote and Sancho Panza and beat[14] them silly. They robbed their saddlebags[15] and cracked Don Quixote's basin on a rock before running away.

Sancho Panza cried, "Now we're going to be in big trouble. We'll be wanted[16] men. The Holy Brotherhood[17] Police will be after[18] us!"

8. **unconscious** [ʌnˋkɑːnʃəs] (a.) 無意識的;昏迷的

9. **convict** [ˋkɑnvɪkt] (n.) 服刑囚犯

10. **overtake** [͵ovərˋteɪk] (v.) 突然侵襲;壓倒

11. **freedom** [ˋfriːdəm] (n.) 自由

12. **testify** [ˋtɛstɪfaɪ] (v.) 證明

13. **mistress** [ˋmɪstrɪs] (n.) 女主人

14. **beat** [biːt] (v.) 擊;打

15. **saddlebag** [ˋsædl͵bæg] (n.) 鞍囊

16. **wanted** [ˋwɑːntɪd] (a.) 受通緝的

17. **brotherhood** [ˋbrʌðər͵hʊd] (n.) 兄弟關係

18. **be after** 追逐

A Match.

❶ Sancho Panza •

❷ The convicts •

❸ Don Quixote •

❹ A barber •

• ⓐ wore a wash basin on his head.

• ⓑ thought the windmills were giants.

• ⓒ was a fat farmer who was a total dunce.

• ⓓ walked in a line with heavy chains around their necks and hands.

B Choose the antonyms for each word.

❶ normal

(a) same   (b) unlike   (c) strange

❷ ridiculous

(a) reasonable   (b) wild   (c) weird

❸ contradict

(a) disagree   (b) agree   (c) hate

C Choose the correct answers to the following questions.

❶ Why did Don Quixote begin killing sheep with his lance?

(a) He thought they were evil giants.

(b) Because they would not proclaim the beauty of his lady, Dulcinea del Toboso.

(c) He thought they were warring armies.

❷ What did Don Quixote claim had happened when he attacked the "long armed giants"?

(a) He said an evil wizard flew by on an invisible horse and changed them into windmills.

(b) He said that he knew they were windmills all along.

(c) He said he needed to get a new pair of glasses.

D Rearrange the sentences in chronological order.

❶ The convicts beat and robbed Don Quixote and Sancho Panza.

❷ Four soldiers herded a dozen men with heavy chains.

❸ The convicts escaped and overtook the soldiers.

❹ Don Quixote hit the sergeant on the head with his lance.

❺ Sancho told Don Quixote that the prisoners were dangerous convicts who needed to be punished.

_____ ⇨ _____ ⇨ _____ ⇨ _____ ⇨ _____

The Rise and Fall of Chivalry

The idea of chivalry is closely associated with[1] the rise of the medieval[2] knight. With his heavy armor, lance, and sword, the knight had become the most awesome[3] force on the battlefield.

Some scholars claim that chivalry evolved[4] from the German tribes[5] in which the bravest warriors[6] were chosen to be companions and guardians of their king. However, these early German knights did not believe in defending the weak, which was one of the main ideals of chivalry.

It wasn't until the 11th century that the code of chivalry was established[7]: "to speak the truth, to help the oppressed[8] and weak, and to never turn back from the enemy." This code quickly spread throughout Europe.

1. **be associated with** 與……相關
2. **medieval** [ˌmediˈiːvəl] (a.) 中世紀的
3. **awesome** [ˈɔːsəm] (a.) 可怕的
4. **evolve** [ɪˈvɑːlv] (v.) 演變
5. **tribe** [traɪb] (n.) 部落；種族
6. **warrior** [ˈwɔːriər] (n.) 戰士；勇士

This romantic ideal appealed to[9] the women of the time, and since they were considered[10] the "weaker sex," knights would swear to protect them from danger. From this evolved the idea of a strong, handsome champion who would undergo[11] very difficult tasks to win his lady's love.

With changing military tactics[12] and new inventions[13], however, knights lost their influence. As the influence of the knights declined[14], so did the ideals of chivalry.

Literature[15], which had once greatly praised chivalry, now made fun of its failings. The best example of this was Cervantes' novel "Don Quixote." Chivalry survived only as a romantic ideal of proper behavior for gentlemen. Finally, when women asserted[16] their equality[17] and demanded that men treat them as equals, popular authors claimed that "chivalry was dead."

7. **establish** [ɪ`stæblɪʃ] (v.) 建立；制定
8. **oppressed** [ə`prest] (a.) 受迫害的
9. **appeal to** 對……有吸引力
10. **consider** [kən`sɪdɚ] (v.) 認為
11. **undergo** [ˌʌndɚ`gou] (v.) 經歷
12. **tactics** [`tæktɪks] (n.) 策略；手段
13. **invention** [ɪn`venʃən] (n.) 發明
14. **decline** [dɪ`klaɪn] (v.) 衰退
15. **literature** [`lɪtərətʃʊr] (n.) 文學
16. **assert** [ə`sɜːrt] (v.) 聲稱；維護
17. **equality** [ɪ`kwɑːləti] (n.) 平等；相等

Chapter Three

The Giant Killer

To escape from the Holy Brotherhood, Don Quixote and Sancho Panza fled[1] into the mountains. They traveled high up to a desolate[2] lonely country of the Sierra Moreno range[3].

"All great men go through[4] a period of despair when they question everything they believe in[5]," Don Quixote said. He turned to his hungry squire, "I am sending you to El Toboso, with a message of my love for Dulcinea. She must tell me whether she can return my love or not. I will stay here and whip myself until you return."

All Sancho could think about was the feast he was going to eat as soon as he got back to a village.

1. **flee** [fliː] (v.) 逃走 (flee-fled-fled)
2. **desolate** [ˋdesələt] (a.) 荒涼的
3. **range** [reɪndʒ] (n.) 山脈
4. **go through** 通過；接受
5. **believe in** 確信；信奉
6. **take off** 脫下
7. **chest** [tʃest] (n.) 胸膛
8. **branch** [bræntʃ] (n.) 樹枝
9. **scene** [siːn] (n.) 景色
10. **call to** 呼喚
11. **overdo** [ˌoʊvərˋduː] (v.) 做得過分

"Ride quickly, Sancho Panza," commanded Don Quixote as he took off[6] his armor. Then he smashed himself in the chest[7] with a large rock and began to beat himself on the back with a tree branch[8].

Riding away from the strange scene[9], Sancho called to[10] his master, "Don't overdo[11] it, or there'll be nothing left of you before I can return."

Check Up True or False.

☐T ☐F   1. Don Quixote sent Sancho to a village to get some food.

☐T ☐F   2. Sancho laughed at the self-torture of his master.

Ans: 1. F 2. F

18

Halfway to[1] the village, Sancho stopped at[2] an inn for the feast he had been waiting for. As he approached the door after his big meal, he came face to face with Don Quixote's old friends, the priest and the barber.

"Hey, you work for our troubled friend, Senor Quixano, don't you?" the priest said to Sancho.

"It's true. I am his squire."

"How can you believe his nonsense[3]? Don't you realize he has lost his mind[4]?"

"There have been some strange things happening," replied Sancho.

"Where is he now?" demanded the barber.

"He's in the mountains, waiting for me to return with an answer from his mistress, the lady Dulcinea del Toboso."

"Her answer to what?" asked the priest.

"Something about love," answered Sancho.

"Take us to[5] him. We have to bring him back to the village with us," said the priest.

"I will, but I warn you he'll never come back with you."

"Hmm," said the barber, "I have a plan. I'll be back in a minute."

Shortly after[6], the barber came back with two dresses from the innkeeper's wife.

✓Check Up Fill in the blanks.

The priest and the barber thought that Don Quixote had
_____ _____ _____. (= go crazy)

Ans: lost his mind

1. **halfway to**
   在前往……的半路
2. **stop at** 中途停在
3. **nonsense** ['nɑːnsens] (n.)
   胡說；胡鬧
4. **lose one's mind**
   失去理智
5. **take A to B** 帶某人到某地
6. **shortly after** 不久

19

The three traveled back to the mountains. That night, they camped[1] and discussed the details[2] of their plan. In the morning, Sancho went off to find Don Quixote and tell him about the ladies in need of help. Meanwhile[3], the priest and the barber put on the dresses and began cooking bacon over the fire for their breakfast. As they ate and talked, they saw a beautiful woman passing by.

"We must show ourselves at once," said the priest. They stepped out to meet her.

The girl screamed when she saw them, and tried to run away.

"Do not fear us," shouted the priest, "I am a man of God!"

"If you're a priest, why are you wearing that dress?" she questioned.

"It's a long story," he replied.

"By the way[4], why are you wandering[5] these hills?" asked the barber.

The beautiful young girl then told her sad story.

1. **camp** [kæmp] (v.) 露營
2. **detail** [dɪˈteɪl] (n.) 細節
3. **meanwhile** [ˈmiːnwaɪl] (adv.) 同時
4. **by the way** 此外；順帶一提
5. **wander** [ˈwɑːndər] (v.) 漫遊；閒逛
6. **be married to** 與……結婚
7. **duke** [djuːk] (n.) 公爵
8. **brokenhearted** [ˈbroukənˈhɑːrtɪd] (a.) 心碎的

"My name is Dorotea. I am the daughter of a wealthy farmer. I was to be married to[6] the Duke[7]'s son, Ferdinando. But he left me for another woman. I was so brokenhearted[8] that I came here to cry away the rest of my days."

✓*Check Up* Fill in the blanks.

Why were the two men wearing dresses?
→ Because they tried to disguise themselves as ladies
_____ _____ of help.

Ans: in need

One Point Lesson

I was **to** be married to the Duke's son, Ferdinando.
我將要和公爵的兒子費迪南多結婚。

be to：將要……

e.g. He was **to** come back and help me.。
他將要回來幫助我。

🎧 20

Then the priest had an idea. "Perhaps a truly[1] beautiful lady such as[2] yourself could convince Don Quixote to come back to our village, rather than[3] an old priest and barber dressed like women."

Dorotea agreed to[4] their plan and put on one of the dresses.

1. **truly** [`truːli] (adv.) 真正地
2. **such as** 像……這樣
3. **rather than** 而不是
4. **agree to** 同意；接受
5. **lead A to B** 帶……前往
6. **fall to one's knees** 下跪

When Sancho returned, he led them to[5] Don Quixote, who was still lashing himself with the branch of an old olive tree.

Immediately, Dorotea fell to her knees[6]. "Please, brave knight, a terrible giant is attacking my father's kingdom[7]. You must help us!"

"Of course I will help you! Sancho, prepare my horse. We leave at once. I cannot refuse[8] a princess in distress."

Later the group arrived at the inn where Sancho had first met the barber and the priest. The innkeeper ran out to greet[9] them and was met by the priest. The priest handed[10] him ten gold pieces and said, "My friend in the iron suit is mad. He thinks he's a knight and this is a castle. I ask you only to play along[11] for the night and let us stay until morning."

7. **kingdom** [ˈkɪŋdəm] (n.) 王國
8. **refuse** [rɪˈfjuːz] (v.) 拒絕
9. **greet** [griːt] (v.) 問候
10. **hand** [hænd] (v.) 遞交
11. **play along** 合作；配合演出

21

"Yes, my wife heard something about a lunatic[1] roaming[2] the valley," said the innkeeper. "I heard the Holy Brotherhood is searching for him. You may stay, but your crazy friend will have to stay in the hayloft[3] where I keep my wine, so he won't bother anyone."

The priest and barber agreed.

Long past midnight, after everyone had gone to bed, the priest awoke to the loud sound of gushing[4] liquid, as if a river had burst into[5] the inn. Suddenly, Sancho Panza stumbled into the room, covered in blood. "My master is fighting a giant upstairs! It's a blood bath[6] up there!"

The priest helped him up and tasted some of the redness[7] on his fingers. "Sancho, this isn't blood, you simpleton[8]. It's wine!"

1. **lunatic** [ˋluːnətɪk] (n.) 精神錯亂的人
2. **roam** [roʊm] (v.) 漫步；漫遊
3. **hayloft** [ˋheɪlɑːft] (n.) 秣草棚
4. **gush** [gʌʃ] (v.) 冒出；湧出
5. **burst into** 情緒突然發作
6. **blood bath** 大屠殺
7. **redness** [ˋrednɪs] (n.) 紅色
8. **simpleton** [ˋsɪmpəltən] (n.) 傻瓜
9. **sprint** [sprɪnt] (v.) 奮力跑
10. **shudder** [ˋʃʌdər] (v.) 發抖

Sprinting[9] up the stairs, the priest shuddered[10] when he saw what had happened. There was Don Quixote, swinging his sword and stabbing[11] the huge pigskin[12] sacks[13] full of wine hung[14] from the ceiling.

"Ah ha!" cried Don Quixote as the wine splashed[15] out over him, blinding his eyes. "Another fatal[16] wound. Soon there will be no more blood left in your body. Victory will be mine!"

11. **stab** [stæb] (v.) 刺；刺傷
12. **pigskin** [ˈpɪɡˌskɪn] (n.) 豬皮革
13. **sack** [sæk] (n.) 袋；麻袋
14. **hang** [hæŋ] (v.) 懸掛 (hang-hung-hung)
15. **splash** [splæʃ] (v.) 潑；潑濕
16. **fatal** [ˈfeɪtl] (a.) 致命的

22

The innkeeper raced[1] upstairs screaming, "Oh no, you're a madman. My best wine is all gone. My wife has sent for the Holy Brotherhood. You'll pay for all of this damage!"

As the officers[2] of the Holy Brotherhood arrived to arrest[3] Don Quixote, the priest came and took one of the officers aside for a moment. He explained that Don Quixote was crazy and needed to be taken home for medical[4] attention[5]. The priest also told the officer to have his men put some chalk on their faces.

1. **race** [reɪs] (v.) 疾走
2. **officer** [ˋɔːfɪsər] (n.) 警官
3. **arrest** [əˋrest] (v.) 逮捕
4. **medical** [ˋmedɪkəl] (a.) 醫療的
5. **attention** [əˋtenʃən] (n.) 照顧
6. **slay** [sleɪ] (v.) 殺死
   (slay-slew-slain)
7. **be surrounded by** 被……包圍
8. **ghostly** [ˋgoʊstli] (a.) 鬼似的
9. **figure** [ˋfɪgjər] (n.) 人物；人影
10. **demon** [ˋdiːmən] (n.) 魔鬼
11. **struggle to** 掙扎；努力
12. **strength** [strenθ] (n.) 力量；力氣

Soon after, Dorotea came to Don Quixote. "Brave knight, you have slain[6] the giant and saved my father's kingdom. I thank you."

"It was my pleasure, dear princess," said Don Quixote.

Suddenly the knight was surrounded by[7] eight ghostly[8] figures[9] with white faces.

One of them stepped forward and said,

"We are demons[10], sent by the evil wizard to take you back to your village! Get into this cage!"

Don Quixote tried to fight, but the eight men seized him and locked him into the cage. Don Quixote struggled to[11] break free from the cage until his strength[12] was gone. Then he fell asleep.

✓Check Up True or False.

☐T ☐F 1. Don Quixote needed to have some medical care.

☐T ☐F 2. The officers disguised themselves as knights to capture Don Quixote.

Ans: 1. T 2. F

A Match.

1 Dorotea •

2 Don Quixote •

3 The innkeeper •

4 The priest •

• a Sancho, this isn't blood, you simpleton. It's wine!

• b You saved my father's kingdom. Thank you.

• c I cannot refuse a princess in distress.

• d My best wine is all gone!

B Fill in the blanks with given words.

lunatic   feast   fled   greet   gushing

1 Don Quixote and Sancho Panza _____ into the mountains.

2 Long past midnight, the priest awoke to the loud sound of _____ liquid.

3 Yes, my wife heard something about a _____ roaming the valley.

4 Sancho stopped at an inn for the _____ he had been waiting for.

5 The innkeeper ran out to _____ them and was met by the priest.

C Choose the correct answer.

1 Why did Don Quixote stab the wineskins?

(a) Because he hated wine.

(b) Because he wanted to drink the wine.

(c) Because he thought the wineskins were a giant and the wine was his blood.

2 What did the Holy Brotherhood officers do before they captured Don Quixote?

(a) They asked him a lot of questions.

(b) They rubbed chalk on their faces so he would think they were demons.

(c) They did a funny dance.

D True or False.

T F **1** Don Quixote decided to whip himself until Sancho returned with an answer from Dulcinea.

T F **2** Sancho would not tell the priest and the barber of Don Quixote's secret location.

T F **3** Dorotea was to be married to the duke's son, but he left her.

T F **4** The innkeeper was happy that Don Quixote stabbed his wineskins.

A New Quest[1]

Don Quixote stayed in bed for several weeks. His niece and housekeeper watched him closely, hoping his knightly[2] madness[3] was finished.

One day, the barber and the priest visited him.

"I'm fully recovered[4] and ready to get back to my old life," said Don Quixote.

"So old friend," asked the priest, "what do you think our king should do about this Turkish sultan[5] who has threatened to attack our shores[6]?"

---

1. **quest** [kwest] (n.) 探索
2. **knightly** [ˋnaɪtli] (a.) 騎士的
3. **madness** [ˋmædnɪs] (n.) 瘋狂
4. **recover** [rɪˋkʌvər] (v.) 恢復
5. **sultan** [ˋsʌltən] (n.) 蘇丹
6. **shores** [ʃɔr] (n.)
   沿海國家;沿海地區
7. **joust** [dʒaʊst] (v.) 騎馬比武
8. **contest** [ˋkɑːntest] (n.)
   比賽;競爭
9. **courageous** [kəˋreɪdʒəs] (a.)
   英勇的;勇敢的
10. **demonstrate** [ˋdemənstreɪt]
    (v.) 示範操作
11. **the forces** 軍隊武力
12. **employ** [ɪmˋplɔɪ] (v.) 僱用
13. **squeezed** [skwiːz] (v.)
    擠著行進
14. **grin** [grɪn] (n.) 露齒的笑

"I would hold a jousting[7] contest[8] to find the bravest knight in all of Spain," said Don Quixote. "Then I would send that single courageous[9] knight to conquer the sultan's armies."

Don Quixote sat up in bed, demonstrating[10] the sword thrusts to destroy the sultan's forces[11].

"Oh dear," said the barber to the priest, "it seems as if our friend's sanity has not returned. We may have to employ[12] more shocking tactics to bring his mind back."

Suddenly Sancho squeezed[13] into the room with a grin[14] on his face and gave the old knight some good news.

"Last night I was at a party to welcome back young Carrasco, who has been studying at Salamanca University. Before I could say 'hello,' he told me he had read about all of our adventures," said Sancho. "Somebody wrote a book called *Don Quixote*, and it's the biggest bestseller in all of Spain!"

"Bring him to me, my squire. I must meet this young man," said Don Quixote.

1. **chubby** [ˋtʃʌbi] (a.) 圓圓胖胖的
2. **expression** [ɪkˋsprɛʃən] (n.) 表情
3. **youth** [juːθ] (n.) 年輕人
4. **humble** [ˋhʌmbəl] (v.) 使謙卑
5. **presence** [ˋprɛzəns] (n.) 出席；存在
6. **extraordinary** [ɪkˋstrɔːrdəneri] (a.) 非凡的
7. **beloved** [bɪˋlʌvɪd] (a.) 心愛的；親愛的
8. **class** [klæs] (n.) 階級
9. **author** [ˋɔːθər] (n.) 作者
10. **hop** [hɑːp] (v.) 單足跳；跳越

A few minutes later, Sancho returned, leading a young man with a chubby[1] face and a mischievous expression[2] into the room. Before Don Quixote could speak, the youth[3] fell onto his knees and said, "Oh, great knight, I'm humbled[4] to be in your excellent presence[5]!"

Carrasco kept talking, trying to control his giggles. "In all the history of chivalry, no one can find a braver, more extraordinary[6] knight than Don Quixote. The book is beloved[7] by every man and woman in every social class[8]. The author[9] is even talking about writing part two!"

"Well, then," cried Don Quixote, hopping[10] out of bed, "it's time to get back in the saddle. My public needs me!"

One Point Lesson

In all the history of chivalry, no one can find a **braver, more extraordinary** knight **than** Don Quixote.
在騎士歷史中，再也找不到比唐吉訶德更勇敢不凡的騎士了。

比較級 + than：比……更……

Nothing is **more comfortable than** this old chair.
沒有什麼比這張舊椅子更加舒適的了。

🎧 25

Seven days later, Don Quixote and Sancho Panza saddled their mounts[1] and prepared to ride. Carrasco was there to wish them farewell[2].

Suddenly the housekeeper and niece burst out of[3] the house and cried, "What's going on here? Where's the priest? He must stop this madness!"

Carrasco whispered[4] to them, "Don't worry. The priest and I have a plan to bring him home. You'll see in a day or two."

---

1. **mount** [maʊnt] (n.) 坐騎
2. **farewell** [`fer`wel] (n.) 告別
3. **burst out of** 從……衝出

4. **whisper** [`wɪspər] (v.) 低聲說
5. **ride off** 離開

Then Don Quixote shouted farewell, and they rode off[5].

"So what's our first move?" asked Sancho after they had been riding for an hour.

"We are riding to El Toboso where you will guide me to the palace of my mistress."

"Oh no," fretted[6] Sancho. "I'm not sure I can remember where she lives."

Later they found themselves riding around the dark streets of El Toboso, hopelessly[7] lost. Sancho convinced Don Quixote that they should wait until morning to find Dulcinea. After eating breakfast at their campsite[8], Sancho rode off, trying to figure out[9] what to do.

√Check Up Choose the correct answer.

Sancho worried that _____.
Ⓐ Carrasco had a plot to harm his master's reputation
Ⓑ Don Quixote would leave him alone in El Toboso
Ⓒ he could not find the place where Dulcinea lived

Ans: C

---

6. **fret** [fret] (v.) 苦惱；發愁
7. **hopelessly** [ˋhoʊpləsli] (adv.) 無可救藥地
8. **campsite** [ˋkæmpsaɪt] (n.) 野營地
9. **figure out** 想出

As he was trying to think of a solution[1], Sancho saw three peasant girls riding across the plain on donkeys. He had an idea. He turned around and rode back to camp.

"Master, I have great news," he cried.

"Will she allow me to visit?" Don Quixote asked hopefully.

"Polish[2] your suit. She couldn't wait for your visit. She's riding here with two of her maids[3]."

Don Quixote ran around in a panic[4]. Sancho helped him into his armor, and minutes later they were riding through the trees.

"Where is she?" cried Don Quixote.

"Over there," said Sancho, pointing to the peasant girls who were riding past.

"All I see are three ugly girls on donkeys," said Don Quixote.

"But sir, those are the prettiest women I've ever seen."

Don Quixote walked up to them and asked the one in the middle, "Are you my mistress,

1. **solution** [sə`luːʃən] (n.) 解決辦法
2. **polish** [`poʊlɪʃ] (v.) 擦亮
3. **maid** [meɪd] (n.) 侍女
4. **in a panic** 處於驚恐
5. **let out** 發出
6. **waste** [weɪst] (v.) 浪費

Princess? Are you Dulcinea, the sweetest rose in Spain?"

The girl let out[5] a big laugh, "Sorry, Granddad, I can't waste[6] time talking with lunatics."

Then she kicked Sancho so hard he almost fell off his donkey. The girls rode off, leaving Don Quixote in a cloud of dust.

> One Point Lesson

But, sir, those are **the prettiest women I've ever seen.**
但是，先生，那些是我看過最漂亮的女人了。

最高級：代表最極端的。用 most + 形容詞或是字尾加 est 或 iest。

e.g This is **the most interesting story I've ever heard.**
這是我聽過最有趣的故事了。

🎧 27

"The evil wizard has changed my love into a disgusting[1] country wench[2]!" cried Don Quixote.

"It's terrible," cried Sancho, clapping his hands with glee[3] because his plan was working so well[4].

---

1. **disgusting** [dɪsˋgʌstɪŋ] (a.)
   極糟的；令人作嘔的
2. **country wench** 鄉下姑娘
3. **glee** [gliː] (n.) 快樂
4. **work well** 運作良好
5. **strike** [straɪk] (v.) 打；擊
   (strike-struck-struck/
   stricken)

"Now I am truly the Knight of the Long Face. This evil wizard has struck[5] me in my weakest spot[6]! I must find a way to break his spell and restore[7] her beauty!"

Don Quixote spent the rest of that day crying in the woods, reciting[8] poetry about lost love. Sancho contented himself with[9] two salamis and a leather cask[10] of wine.

Suddenly Don Quixote hissed[11], "I hear two men approaching in the forest."

"Where?" asked Sancho.

"On the other side of those bushes[12]."

Then the two sat and listened.

"My lady, Casilda, is the most lovely woman in Spain!" said the voice. "And she has sent me, the Knight of the Forest, on my mission to destroy all knights who would disagree."

"This knight lies," whispered Don Quixote.

6. **spot** [spɑːt] (n.)
   污點；處境
7. **restore** [rɪˋstɔːr] (v.) 恢復
8. **recite** [rɪˋsaɪt] (v.)
   背誦；朗誦

9. **content oneself with**
   滿足於
10. **cask** [kæsk] (n.) 一桶
11. **hiss** [hɪs] (v.) 嘶嘶地說出
12. **bush** [bʊʃ] (n.) 灌木叢

"You are mistaken!" shouted Don Quixote, stepping out of the bushes to face the knight. "I must tell you that my Dulcinea is the most beautiful woman on Earth."

"Then we must do battle," the other knight replied coolly[1].

"We will joust at dawn," replied Don Quixote.

"Yes, but there is one condition[2]. The loser[3] must return to his village and swear to stay there and not enter any combat[4] for one year."

"I accept," answered Don Quixote.

The next morning at dawn, the knights met on opposite[5] sides of a clearing[6]. To the left of the Knight of the Forest was his squire, a hunchback[7] with a large purple nose.

Without warning, the Knight of the Forest spurred his steed into a gallop and charged Don Quixote with his lance. Don Quixote immediately raised his lance. At the last moment, the Knight of the Forest's horse neighed[8] and refused to take another step[9]. Don Quixote charged with all his might[10] and knocked the other knight out of his saddle. Don Quixote quickly jumped down from Rocinante, drawing his sword and holding it to the downed knight's neck.

✓Check Up Choose the correct answer.

Why did Don Quixote fight with the Knight of the Forest?

(A) Because he wanted to show off his strength.
(B) Because he did not agree with the other's opinion.
(C) Because he did not want to go back to his village.

Ans: B

1. **coolly** [`kuli] (adv.) 冷漠地
2. **condition** [kən`dɪʃən] (n.)
   情況；條件
3. **loser** [`luːzər] (n.) 輸家
4. **combat** [`kɑːmbæt] (n.)
   戰鬥
5. **opposite** [`ɑːpəzɪt] (a.)
   相反的；對立的

6. **clearing** [`klɪrərɪŋ] (n.)
   林中空地
7. **hunchback** [`hʌntʃbæk]
   (n.) 駝背的人
8. **neigh** [neɪ] (v.) 嘶鳴
9. **take a step** 邁出一步
10. **with all one's might**
    盡其所能

77

🎧 29

"Do you surrender?" Don Quixote demanded.

"Yes," cried the Knight of the Forest, "I'm finished."

Then Don Quixote commanded Sancho to[1] remove[2] the knight's helmet.

"Well," cried Sancho, "this knight looks like that youth Carrasco!"

"Yes, he does," agreed Don Quixote. "The power of this evil wizard to change people's faces is amazing."

1. **command A to do something** 命令某人去做某事
2. **remove** [rɪˈmuːv] (v.) 去掉;除去
3. **enchanter** [ɪnˈtʃæntər] (n.) 巫師
4. **fling off** 脫下
5. **put away** 收起
6. **drag away** 拖走
7. **wheat** [wiːt] (n.) 小麥

"No, I really am Carrasco," sobbed the student.

"It would be safer to kill him now," said Sancho. "That would be one less enchanter[3] to worry about."

Don Quixote raised his sword to strike, but the hunchback rushed over and flung off[4] his robe. It was Don Quixote's friend, the barber. "Put your sword away[5]," he said.

"Amazing," said Don Quixote, "This evil wizard never stops."

The barber dragged Carrasco away[6] toward their campsite, cursing him for not being better in a joust.

The next morning found Don Quixote and Sancho Panza riding through a wheat[7] field. The victory over the Knight of the Forest left Don Quixote feeling unstoppable[8]. He didn't suspect for a moment that it had been a plot[9] hatched[10] by the priest to bring him back to the village.

8. **unstoppable** [ʌnˈstɑːpəbəl] (a.) 無法遏止的

9. **plot** [plɑːt] (n.) 陰謀；情節

10. **hatch** [hætʃ] (v.) 策劃

30

Stepping onto the road, the knight and his squire came upon[1] a royal[2] cart. Raising his lance, Don Quixote blocked the cart and said, "Halt, or I'll slice[3] you in two. I demand to know what you have in this cart."

"A lion," called one of the cart drivers, "A gift to our king from an African prince."

"Dangerous?" asked Don Quixote.

"It's thirsty for[4] blood. It's even more dangerous because it's hungry. So clear off[5], old man, before you get hurt[6]."

"I am Don Quixote," proclaimed the knight. "And I'm not afraid of any pussycats[7]!"

Then he swung his lance below the driver's nose. "Open the cage!"

1. **come upon** 碰上
2. **royal** [ˈrɔɪəl] (a.) 王室的
3. **slice** [slaɪs] (v.) 切
4. **be thirsty for** 渴望得到
5. **clear off** 逃離
6. **get hurt** 受傷
7. **pussycat** 貓
8. **mate** [meɪt] (n.) 同伴;配偶
9. **position oneself** 使處於……
10. **reconsider** [ˌriːkənˈsɪdər] (v.) 重新考慮
11. **gigantic** [dʒaɪˈgæntɪk] (a.) 巨大的;龐大的
12. **stick** [stɪk] (v.) 卡住
13. **jaw** [dʒɔː] (n.) 顎;下頜;下巴
14. **drool** [druːl] (n.) 口水
15. **curve** [kɜːrv] (v.) 使彎曲
16. **blaze** [bleɪz] (v.) 閃耀

Sancho and the driver's mate[8] quickly ran up a nearby hill, while Don Quixote positioned himself[9] in front of the lion's cage, and the driver prepared to pull a rope that would open it.

"Will you reconsider[10]?" asked the driver.

"Don Quixote does not fear danger!" shouted the knight. "Pull!"

The door crashed open, and a gigantic[11] lion stuck[12] his head into the air. His jaws[13] were black and covered with thick drool[14], his teeth yellow and curved[15] like knives. The lion's eyes blazed[16] as if on fire.

31

"I'm waiting for you, King of the jungle," Don Quixote cried fearlessly[1]. "Are you afraid to come out?"

The lion stared at the old knight for a moment, and then yawned[2] and went to sleep.

"This lion is a coward[3]!" shouted Don Quixote. "Driver, rattle[4] his cage. Make him roar[5]!"

"I will not!" replied the driver, dropping the rope that closed the lion's cage. "You are the bravest man in Spain. No one else would go up against a man-killer."

"Will you swear to our king?" asked Don Quixote.

"He will receive a full report of your bravery," replied the driver.

Don Quixote signaled to[6] Sancho and the driver's mate that it was safe to return.

---

1. **fearlessly** [ˋfɪrːlɪsli] (adv.) 無畏地
2. **yawn** [jɔːn] (v.) 打哈欠
3. **coward** [ˋkaʊərd] (n.) 懦夫
4. **rattle** [ˋrætl] (v.) 晃動
5. **roar** [rɔːr] (v.) 吼叫
6. **signal to** 向……比手勢

"From this day on," announced Don Quixote, "I wish to be known as the Knight of the Lions. Men will tell tales of this adventure hundreds of years to come!"

✔Check Up True or False.

T F 1. Don Quixote professed to be the Knight of the Lions.

T F 2. The king gave Don Quixote a big prize for his bravery.

Ans: 1. T 2. F

A Match.

❶ Carrasco   •

❷ The barber   •

❸ The Knight   •
of the Forest

❹ Don Quixote •

• ⓐ challenged Don Quixote to a joust.

• ⓑ was dressed as a hunchback with a large, purple nose.

• ⓒ was a youth with a chubby face and a mischievous expression.

• ⓓ thought an evil wizard turned his lady into an ugly peasant girl.

B Choose the right underlined word.

❶ (a) "I am Don Quixote!" <u>proclaimed</u> the knight.

  (b) Sancho Panza <u>proclaimed</u> himself into the knight's bedroom.

❷ (a) They began to <u>lance</u> their breakfast on the campfire.

  (b) Don Quixote raised his <u>lance</u>.

❸ (a) She <u>eagered</u> herself in front of the knight.

  (b) Sancho was <u>eager</u> to avoid trouble with strangers.

C Choose the correct answer.

❶ Why did Carrasco pretend to be the Knight of the Forest?

(a) Because he secretly wanted to defeat Don Quixote.

(b) Because the priest had a plan to make Don Quixote return to his village.

(c) Because he also dreamed of being a knight-errant.

❷ What happened when Don Quixote faced the lion?

(a) The lion attacked Don Quixote.

(b) Don Quixote killed the lion.

(c) The lion yawned and went to sleep.

D Rearrange the sentences in chronological order.

❶ Don Quixote knocked the Knight of the Forest out of his saddle with his lance.

❷ The Knight of the Forest surrendered to Don Quixote.

❸ The Knight of the Forest said his lady Casilda was the most beautiful woman.

❹ Don Quixote agreed to the Knight of the Forest's terms.

❺ Don Quixote held his sword to the Knight of the Forest's neck.

_____ ⇨ _____ ⇨ _____ ⇨ _____ ⇨ _____

Dreams vs. Reality

It is surprising that the novel *Don Quixote* is regarded as[1] one of the best novels of all time. Cervantes originally intended it to be just a short comic parody of popular romantic stories about chivalry. The author wanted to make fun of[2] stories that featured[3] gallant knights fighting terrible monsters in an attempt[4] to win their chosen lady's favor.

Cervantes' hero, Don Quixote, is an insane dreamer who looks ridiculous[5] in his homemade armor while riding around on an old horse. His enemies are just figments[6] of his crazed imagination. Most of the early fans of this book regarded it as Cervantes' intended quick, light, and humorous read.

1. **regard *A* as *B*** 將 A 視為 B
2. **make fun of** 取笑；嘲弄
3. **feature** [ˋfiːtʃər] (v.) 以……為特色
4. **attempt** [əˋtempt] (n.) 企圖
5. **ridiculous** [rɪˋdɪkjʊləs] (a.) 滑稽的
6. **figment** [ˋfɪgmənt] (n.) 虛構的事
7. **reverse** [rɪˋvɜːrs] (v.) 顛倒

However, over the years, the public has reversed[7] their opinion of it. If readers look deeper at the main themes of the novel, they can find a warm, human tale of a man who tries to follow his ideals. Don Quixote, the foolish knight, is seen as a symbol of old-

fashioned romantic idealism[8] trying to survive in a world that has become coldly practical[9].

Paying counterpart[10] to Quixote's idealism is his squire, Sancho Panza. Panza symbolizes[11] reality just as his master Quixote represents[12] illusion[13]. But Panza seems just as crazy because he follows Quixote in the hopes of gaining wealth. Although he sees windmills where Quixote sees evil giants, Panza is just as foolish as his master. This makes readers wonder which is more foolish being a dreamer, or being strictly practical?

8. **idealism** [aɪˈdɪəlɪzəm] (n.) 理想主義

9. **practical** [ˈpræktɪkəl] (a.) 實際的；注重實效的

10. **counterpart** [ˈkaʊntərpɑːrt] (n.) 對應的人或物

11. **symbolize** [ˈsɪmbəlaɪz] (v.) 象徵

12. **represent** [ˌreprɪˈzent] (v.) 代表

13. **illusion** [ɪˈluːʒən] (n.) 幻覺

The Final Adventures

Sancho grumbled[1] and sulked[2] for three days as Don Quixote led them through the forest. Their food was almost gone, and the squire had to go to sleep hungry, under a damp[3] blanket worrying about wolves and other predators[4]. Don Quixote was proud of[5] their sufferings[6], often reminding[7] Sancho that "a hard life makes a brave heart."

On the fourth day, at sunset, they came across a group of riders. Among them was a lady dressed in green velvet. She sat atop a majestic[8] white stallion[9] and held a falcon[10] on her arm.

"A huntress[11]," gasped[12] Don Quixote. "Perhaps even a princess. She'll certainly want to be introduced to me."

1. **grumble** [ˋgrʌmbəl] (v.) 咕噥；埋怨
2. **sulk** [sʌlk] (v.) 生悶氣
3. **damp** [dæmp] (a.) 潮濕的

4. **predator** [ˋprɛdətər] (n.) 捕食性動物
5. **be proud of** 以……感到自豪
6. **suffering** [ˋsʌfərɪŋ] (n.) 苦難

"She probably just wants us to mind our own business[13]," Sancho replied with a grin.

Ignoring his squire, the knight commanded him, "Ride over there and introduce me."

Sancho groaned[14] and spurred his donkey in the group's direction.

"My lady," he called. "My master, the Knight of the Lions, formerly[15] known as the Knight of the Long Face, wishes to . . ."

7. **remind** [rɪˋmaɪnd] (v.) 提醒
8. **majestic** [məˋdʒestɪk] (a.) 雄偉的
9. **stallion** [ˋstæljən] (n.) 種馬
10. **falcon** [ˋfælkən] (n.) 隼；獵鷹
11. **huntress** [ˋhʌntrɪs] (n.) 女獵人
12. **gasp** [gæsp] (v.) 喘氣
13. **mind one's business** 少管閒事
14. **groan** [groʊn] (v.) 抱怨
15. **formerly** [ˋfɔːrmərli] (adv.) 從前

33

"Wait," interrupted the lady, "Did you say the Knight of the Long Face?"

"Yes, and I'm his squire, Sancho . . ."

"Panza?" interrupted the lady again with a smile.

"Yes," gulped[1] Sancho. "Do you know about us?"

"Of course," she replied. "I've read the book of your adventures. It's my husband's and my favorite book!"

"Shall I bring him over then?" asked Sancho.

"You must do more than that," said the lady. "You and your master must come to our nearby castle as our distinguished[2] guests of my husband, the Duke."

1. **gulp** [gʌlp] (v.) 倒抽一口氣
2. **distinguished** [dɪˈstɪŋgwɪʃt] (a.) 卓越的
3. **duchess** [ˈdʌtʃɪs] (n.) 公爵夫人
4. **in truth** 事實上
5. **dim-witted** [ˈdɪmwɪtɪd] (a.) 愚笨的
6. **sidekick** [ˈsaɪdˌkɪk] (n.) 助手
7. **drawbridge** [ˈdrɑːbrɪdʒ] (n.) 吊橋
8. **opulent** [ˈɑːpjʊlənt] (n.) 富麗的
9. **surround** [səˈraʊnd] (v.) 圍繞
10. **fan** [fæn] (v.) 吹
11. **jar** [dʒɑːr] (n.) 罐；罈

The Duchess[3] giggled when Sancho accepted her invitation. In truth[4], she and her husband thought the book Don Quixote was the finest comedy ever written. She and her husband were great jokers, and she figured they would be able to have some fun with the crazy knight and his dim-witted[5] sidekick[6].

The group with Don Quixote and Sancho soon crossed a drawbridge[7] and found themselves inside a vast, opulent[8] castle. Two trumpeters sounded the knight's arrival, and a group of maidens surrounded[9] them, fanning[10] jars[11] of perfume.

Check Up Fill in the blanks.

The Duchess invited Don Quixote and Sancho to have _____ with them.

Ans: fun

34

That night, the knight and his squire ate the best meal of their lives while chatting[1] with their hosts.

The Duke and Duchess listened with great interest about all of their recent adventures. But their greatest interest was in hearing news of Dulcinea.

When they asked about Dulcinea, the knight replied sadly, "My beautiful lady has been transformed into[2] a vulgar[3], donkey-riding trollop[4] by an evil wizard."

1. **chat** [tʃæt] (v.) 聊天；閒談
2. **transform A into B**
   將 A 變成 B
3. **vulgar** [`vʌlgər] (a.)
   粗俗的；通俗的
4. **trollop** [`trɑːləp] (n.)
   邋遢女人；蕩婦

"How terrible!" gasped the Duchess, barely[5] able to contain her laughter.

The next day, the Duke and Duchess convinced Don Quixote to accompany them on a wild boar[6] hunt in the forest. But they had made secret plans to play a big joke on the knight and his squire.

While they were hunting, there was a sudden noise coming through the trees.

"My men must have found a boar. It's coming toward us. Beware[7] its tusks[8]!" said the Duchess.

But when the trees parted, there was no wild boar. Rather, a black stallion came prancing[9] and kicking before them. On its back rode a man, covered in twigs[10], leaves, and ivy.

5. **barely** [ˋberli] (adv.)
   幾乎無法
6. **boar** [bɔːr] (n.) 野豬
7. **beware** [bɪˋwer] (v.)
   小心；提防

8. **tusk** [tʌsk] (n.) 長牙
9. **prance** [præns] (v.) 騰躍
10. **twig** [twɪg] (n.) 細枝

🎧 35

"I am the forest sprite[1]!" the strange figure wearing a green mask with horns on top of[2] his head shouted. "The demons of the forest have sent me with a message for the knight-errant, Don Quixote de La Mancha!"

"I am Don Quixote," replied the knight.

"To free your lady from[3] their spell," the sprite continued, "you must do two things. First of all, your squire must lash himself."

1. **sprite** [spraɪt] (n.) 小精靈
2. **on top of** 在……上面
3. **free A from B**
   使 A 從 B 獲得自由

"How many times?" screamed Sancho.

"Three thousand, three hundred times."

Sancho gasped in disbelief[4].

"But first, you must ride a flying horse through the air and over the mountains. This horse waits for you at the Duke's castle. If you are brave enough to perform these two tasks, your beloved Dulcinea will be set free[5]," said the forest sprite.

Then the creature turned and rode away.

"It's a miracle!" cried the Duchess, "We must return to the castle at once!"

"Yes, but first, Sancho, fetch[6] me a whip," shouted Don Quixote. "You can begin lashing yourself while we ride!"

The terrified[7] squire had already ridden away from the knight's grasp[8].

---

4. **in disbelief** 不可置信
5. **set *A* free** 釋放 A
6. **fetch** [fetʃ] (v.) 拿來
7. **terrified** [ˈterɪfaɪd] (a.) 害怕的
8. **grasp** [græsp] (n.) 控制；支配

Back at the castle, the servants were rushing[1] around, shouting alarm from the towers. There was a giant wooden horse in the middle of the courtyard. The servants told the Duke it had suddenly and mysteriously[2] dropped from the sky. Meanwhile, Don Quixote and Sancho were arguing about[3] the lashes the squire must suffer to free Dulcinea.

"I won't do it," cried the squire.

"For the sake of[4] my lady, I beg you," sobbed the knight.

The Duchess approached them. "You two must cease[5] your squabbling[6]," she said, leading them into the courtyard. She was enjoying every moment of this grand practical joke[7] she had planned with her husband.

Don Quixote stared up at the wooden horse in amazement[8].

"What a creature! It must be twenty feet tall!"

1. **rush** [rʌʃ] (v.) 倉促行動
2. **mysteriously** [mɪˋstɪriəsli] (adv.) 不可思議地
3. **argue about** 爭論
4. **for the sake of** 為了……起見
5. **cease** [siːs] (v.) 停止
6. **squabbling** [ˋskwɑːbəlɪŋ] (n.) 爭吵
7. **practical joke** 惡作劇
8. **in amazement** 驚訝地
9. **rope ladder** 繩梯
10. **trouser** [ˋtraʊzər] (n.) 褲子

Sancho's knees knocked together in fear. There was a rope ladder[9] on the side, which they climbed up. Seeing them mount the wooden horse, the Duke and Duchess could hardly control their laughter.

When the two seated themselves on top of the horse, Sancho found there was nothing to hold on to. So he grabbed onto Don Quixote's trouser[10] belt with both hands.

"There's a carving[1] in the wood here!" exclaimed Don Quixote. "It says we have to blindfold[2] ourselves. Anyone who rides this magic horse without a blindfold will be struck dead!"

1. **carving** [`kɑːrvɪŋ] (n.) 雕刻
2. **blindfold** [`blaɪndfoʊld] (v.) 矇住眼睛
3. **tear** [tɪr] (v.) 撕開 (tear-tore-torn)
4. **smelly** [`smeli] (a.) 有難聞氣味的
5. **squeal** [skwiːl] (v.) 發生笑聲
6. **tap on** 輕拍
7. **lift** [lɪft] (v.) 舉起；提高

"I've got a handkerchief!" said Sancho.

He pulled out his handkerchief, tore[3] it in two, and gave half to his master. The two fixed the smelly[4] halves of handkerchief around their faces. From a balcony above, the Duchess and Duke squealed[5] with pleasure at the sight of the two fools on the horse.

Once their eyes were covered, a servant tapped on[6] the horse, and the servants inside lifted[7] it three feet off the ground and rocked it from side to side.

"We're up in the clouds, Sancho," cried Don Quixote.

"I'm feeling airsick[8]," moaned[9] Sancho.

On a balcony across from the knight and squire, four maidens were pumping a pair of bellows[10] and dousing[11] them with cups of water.

"Hold on, Sancho. We're flying through a rainstorm[12]!" called Don Quixote.

Check Up Fill in the blanks.

The servants' _____ the horse made Don Quixote feel like he was _____.

A flying B tapping C rocking

Ans: C, A

---

8. **airsick** [ˋɛrˏsɪk] (n.) 暈機
9. **moan** [moʊn] (v.) 嗚咽
10. **(a pair of) bellows** （一對）風箱
11. **douse** [daʊs] (v.) 往⋯⋯撥水
12. **rainstorm** [ˋreɪnˏstɔːrm] (n.) 暴風雨

38

At this point, the Duke and Duchess were laughing their socks off[1]. But they were also beginning to feel guilty[2] for playing such a prank on[3] the good knight. The Duke signaled to his butler[4] for the grand finale[5].

A servant lit the horse's tail on fire. There was a "POP" and a "FIZZ" as hundreds of fireworks hidden inside the tail exploded. Sancho wrapped his arms around[6] the knight and howled[7], "Save me, Master. I promise I'll suffer the lashing!"

"All of them?" asked Don Quixote.

"Every one!" cried Sancho.

Then Don Quixote beat the top of the horse with his fist[8]. But this only made the men inside rock it harder. Finally, they tilted[9] it too far, and the wooden horse crashed to the ground. Sancho and the knight were thrown to safety, landing on the soft grass of the castle lawn. Quickly the servants carried the horse away.

---

1. **laugh one's socks off** 笑到欲罷不能
2. **feel guilty** 感到內疚
3. **play a prank on** 耍某人
4. **butler** [ˋbʌtlər] (n.) 男管家
5. **finale** [fɪˋnælɪ] (n.) 結尾
6. **wrap around** 伸展至兩邊
7. **howl** [haʊl] (v.) 號啕大哭

By the time Don Quixote and Sancho tore the rags[10] from their eyes, they were facing the Duchess who leaned over[11] them, acting concerned.

"Welcome back," she said softly, "You've been gone for hours. We were so worried. How was the ride?"

8. **fist** [fɪst] (n.) 拳頭
9. **tilt** [tɪlt] (v.) 使傾斜
10. **rag** [ræg] (n.) 碎布
11. **lean over** 將身體傾向……

39

Sancho and Don Quixote rested for a few days. Then the knight announced it was time for them to leave.

"But what about Sancho's lashing?" asked the Duchess, who didn't want to miss out on[1] the spectacle[2].

"He'll have to carry out[3] the lashes while we travel. Life at court[4] is softening my sword arm[5]. It is time for us to go. I thank you for your hospitality[6]."

Don Quixote and Sancho Panza rode away toward the sea and the city of Barcelona.

The next morning, Don Quixote told Sancho, "I want to see you do some whipping right now."

"Don't rush me," cried Sancho, jumping to his feet[7]. "And I prefer to[8] perform my lashing in private[9]."

1. **miss out on** 錯過
2. **spectacle** [ˋspɛktəkəl] (n.) 場面
3. **carry out** 完成
4. **at court** 在宮廷
5. **sword arm** 右臂
6. **hospitality** [ˌhɑːspɪˋtæləti] (n.) 殷勤招待
7. **jump to one's feet** 一跳而起
8. **prefer to** 比較喜歡
9. **in private** 私底下
10. **shirk** [ʃɜːrk] (v.) 逃避
11. **stomp** [stɑːmp] (v.) 邁著沈重的腳步
12. **unbutton** [ʌnˋbʌtn] (v.) 解開鈕釦

"I don't care how you do it, but I want to hear each lash so I know you're not shirking[10]."

"Fine," snapped Sancho, "I'll get started."

He grabbed the whip and stomped[11] off into the trees. Then he unbuttoned[12] his shirt and cracked the whip against the trunk of the tree.

"Ow!" he yelled. "That one almost drew blood!"

Check Up Fill in the blanks.

Sancho wanted to do his lashing in _____.

Ans: private

103

A few days later, when Don Quixote and
Sancho rode into Barcelona, word had already
spread of their arrival.

The streets were filled with[1] citizens trying
to get a glimpse of[2] the crazy yet noble knight.
People threw flowers and cheered[3]. The leader
of their escort[4] allowed Don Quixote and
Sancho to stay in his luxurious[5] villa[6] in the
middle of the city.

For two weeks they lived like kings. They were paid daily visits by generals, admirals[7], and high-ranking public officials[8].

Each morning, Don Quixote would take Rocinante for a trot[9] along the beach. Then one day, as he was on his morning jaunt[10], he saw a figure approaching him from down the beach. The figure was a knight, wearing a full suit of armor with his visor lowered. When Don Quixote neared the knight, he could see a white crescent[11] emblem[12] on his chest.

"Halt, the Knight of the Lions!" called the Knight of the White Moon. "I have a challenge for you."

1. **be filled with** 充滿
2. **get a glimpse of** 看一眼
3. **cheer** [tʃɪr] (v.) 歡呼
4. **escort** [ˋeskɔːt] (n.) 護衛隊
5. **luxurious** [lʌgˋʒʊəriəs] (a.) 豪華的
6. **villa** [ˋvɪlə] (n.) 別墅
7. **admiral** [ˋædmərəl] (n.) 海軍上將
8. **public official** 政府官員
9. **trot** [trɑːt] (n.) 騎馬小跑
10. **jaunt** [dʒɑːnt] (n.) 遊覽
11. **crescent** [ˋkrezənt] (a.) 月形的
12. **emblem** [ˋembləm] (n.) 徽章

41

"Don Quixote is always ready for a challenge," the old hidalgo answered bravely.

"Then we will joust," said the strange knight, raising a shiny[1] new lance.

"Name your terms[2]," called Don Quixote.

"If you win, this fine horse and my new lance are yours. If I am the victor, you must retire from[3] your career as a knight-errant."

"Retire?" cried Don Quixote. "But that is impossible."

"We young knights are tired of[4] you getting all of the public's attention[5]. We want you to return to your village for a year and live a peaceful life."

"I accept your terms!" snapped Don Quixote.

Then both knights turned away from each other and checked their weapons. When they turned, the Knight of the White Moon spurred his horse into a gallop and thrust his lance toward Don Quixote.

1. **shiny** [ˋʃaɪnɪ] (a.) 發光的
2. **terms** [tɝmz] (n.) 〔複〕條件
3. **retire from** 自……退隱
4. **be tired of** 厭倦
5. **attention** [əˋtenʃən] (n.) 注意
6. **shallow** [ˋʃælo] (a.) 淺的
7. **in a flash** 瞬間
8. **dismount** [dɪsˋmaʊnt] (v.) 下馬

He held his lance with such precision that the elderly knight didn't have a chance and was thrown from his saddle. He landed in the shallow[6] water and sand of the beach. In a flash[7], the Knight of the White Moon dismounted[8] and pressed his sword to Don Quixote's neck.

✓Check Up True or False.

[T][F] 1. If Don Quixote loses, he must quit his questing.

[T][F] 2. The Knight of the White Moon's jousting skills were superior.

Ans: 1. T 2. T

42

"You are vanquished[1]. Do you concede[2]?" demanded the Knight of the White Moon.

"But it means the end of my life," sobbed Don Quixote. "Without chivalry, I am nothing."

"You gave your word[3]," snarled[4] the victor.

"I will retire," coughed[5] Don Quixote, "as I promised."

The knight's tears of defeat mixed with[6] the salt water of the waves. "This is the darkest day of all my adventures," he moaned.

But the Knight of the White Moon showed no mercy[7] and rode off on his stallion. The broken hidalgo sat, sobbing in the surf[8].

1. **vanquish** [ˈvæŋkwɪʃ] (v.) 徹底擊敗
2. **concede** [kənˈsiːd] (v.) 承認
3. **give one's word** 保證
4. **snarl** [snɑːrl] (v.) 吼叫
5. **cough** [kɔːf] (v.) 咳嗽
6. **mix with** 混合
7. **mercy** [ˈmɜːrsi] (n.) 慈悲
8. **surf** [sɜːrf] (n.) 激浪
9. **hobble** [ˈhɑːbəl] (n.) 步履蹣跚

Later, Don Quixote hobbled[9] back to town. He never realized that the Knight of the White Moon was actually the youth, Carrasco. In the months since he had been defeated as the Knight of the Forest, he had studied jousting and horsemanship[10]. He was determined to[11] have his revenge on[12] Don Quixote and to return the crazy hidalgo to his friends in the village.

When Sancho heard of Don Quixote's defeat and retirement, he sobbed.

"You can't quit, Sire. Old dogs don't learn new tricks."

"I promised. Now help me take off[13] my armor. I no longer need it."

As the two began their three-day journey home, they lamented[14] their fate.

10. **horsemanship** [ˋhɔːrsmənʃɪp] (n.) 馬術
11. **be determined to** 下定決心
12. **have one's revenge on** 對某人復仇
13. **take off** 脫下
14. **lament** [ləˋment] (v.) 對……感到悲痛

43

One night, the two men made camp[1] by a stream. Sancho had been trying to lift the brokenhearted knight's spirits all day.

"Can I do anything to make you feel better?" he asked.

"If I knew my lady was safe," said Don Quixote, "I might be able to smile again."

So Sancho wandered[2] off into the nearby woods and lashed a tree letting out blood-chilling[3] cries with each crack[4] of the whip. When Sancho had lashed all the bark[5] off the tree, Don Quixote told him he had finished a thousand lashes and he stopped for the day.

"I am proud of you," Don Quixote told him warmly. "If you can manage a thousand per night, Dulcinea will be free by the time we reach our village."

1. **make camp** 紮營
2. **wander** [ˋwɑːndər] (v.) 漫遊
3. **blooding-chilling** [ˋblʌdɪŋ ˋtʃɪlɪŋ] (a.) 令人寒心的
4. **crack** [kræk] (n.) 爆裂聲
5. **bark** [bɑːrk] (n.) 樹皮
6. **pass by** 經過
7. **rack up** 累積
8. **complete** [kəmˋpliːt] (v.) 完成
9. **shake one's hand** 握手

They rode hard each day, passing by[6] many
sights of past adventures. Each night, Sancho
found a suitable tree to whip and rack up[7]
another thousand lashes. On the fourth
morning, he completed[8] the final two hundred
and forty-eight lashes. Don Quixote shook his
hand[9] and promised to double his salary if
they ever went questing again.

44

When Don Quixote rode into the courtyard of his home, the housekeeper dropped her basket of laundry[1] in the dust.

"Master, you're back in one piece[2]," she cried.

"I am weak," whispered Don Quixote, "Sancho, help me to my room."

1. **laundry** [ˋlɔːndrɪ] (n.)
   洗好的衣服
2. **in one piece** 完整無損的
3. **slip into** 潛入
4. **patiently** [ˋpeɪʃəntlɪ] (adv.)
   耐心地

Back in his bed, the old hidalgo slipped into[3] a sleep that lasted for six days. The fever he had gotten grew stronger each day. He cried and moaned in his sleep, as if being haunted by nightmares. Meanwhile, his friends waited patiently[4] by his bedside[5]. After a week, he opened his eyes to see the priest and the barber sitting at the end of his bed.

"I am back," muttered[6] the old knight.

"Don Quixote!" they shouted, rushing to his side.

"My name is Alonso Quixano," said the man in the bed. "I was mad, but now my mind is restored."

"Is it true? Are all your thoughts of chivalry and wizards really gone from your head?" asked the priest.

"They are all gone," he replied softly. "I am sane[7] enough to know that I am dying."

5. **by one's bedside**
   在某人的床邊
6. **mutter** [ˈmʌtər] (v.)
   低聲嘀咕

7. **sane** [seɪn] (a.) 神智正常的

45

The news that the hidalgo was on his deathbed[1] raced around[2] the village. Sancho came running in from the fields where he had been at work. He was shown into the room and knelt down at his former master's side.

"Perhaps you were a little crazy," Sancho sobbed, "but if you were still a knight, you would not die."

"Your friend who was a knight," replied the hidalgo, "is no longer here. You must forget him."

"I cannot," sobbed the squire.

Sancho tried to convince his old friend not to give up the ghost. But the old hidalgo was overcome with[3] fever. Sancho waited at his bedside for three days until finally, the old knight slipped away[4].

1. **on one's deathbed** 臨終
2. **race around** 傳得沸沸揚揚
3. **be overcome with** 被壓倒；被克服
4. **slip away** 死去
5. **accomplish** [əˋkɑːmplɪʃ] (v.) 完成
6. **feat** [fiːt] (n.) 英勇事蹟
7. **ordinary** [ˋɔːrdəneri] (a.) 普通的
8. **rest in peace** 安息
9. **grand** [grænd] (a.) 崇高的

This was the end of the brave knight, Don Quixote de La Mancha. In his madness, he accomplished[5] feats[6] that ordinary[7] men can only dream of. The stories of his amazing adventures have been told for more than four hundred years.

Rest in peace[8], noble Don Quixote. May the questing be grand[9] and the adventures bring you glory. . .

A Match.

1 Sancho Panza •

2 The Duchess •

3 The forest sprite •

4 Don Quixote •

• a I've read the book of your adventures.

• b You can begin lashing yourself while we ride.

• c I promise I'll suffer the lashing!

• d To free your lady from their spell, you must do two things.

B Choose the antonyms for each word.

1 sulked

(a) cheered   (b) cried   (c) poured

2 majestic

(a) rich   (b) opulent   (c) shabby

3 mysteriously

(a) secretively   (b) obviously   (c) quietly

C Choose the correct answers.

1 Why did Don Quixote and Sancho Panza ride the magic horse?

(a) Because the Duke ordered them to ride it.

(b) Because they enjoyed riding magic horses.

(c) To free the lady Dulcinea from the forest demons' spell

2 How did Don Quixote die?

(a) He was killed by the Knight of the White Moon.

(b) His body was overcome by a fever.

(c) The evil wizard cast a spell that killed him.

D True or False.

T F **1** The people of Barcelona were angry when Don Quixote and Sancho Panza rode into town.

T F **2** The Knight of the White Moon was Carrasco.

T F **3** Because Don Quixote lost the joust, he must leave his hometown.

T F **4** Sancho Panza was sad because Don Quixote was dying.

T F **5** Don Quixote's adventures have been told for more than four hundred years.

Appendixes

1 Basic Grammar

> 要增強英文閱讀理解能力，應練習找出英文的主結構。
> 要擁有良好的英語閱讀能力，首先要理解英文的段落結構。

「英文的主要句型結構比較簡單」

　　所有的英文文章都是由主詞和動詞所構成的，無論文章再怎麼長或複雜，它的架構一定是「主詞和動詞」，而「補語」和「受詞」是做補充主詞和動詞的角色。

He knew / that she told a lie / at the party.

他知道　　　　　她說了謊　　　　　在舞會上

⇨ 他知道她在舞會上說謊的事。

As she was walking / in the garden, / she smelled /

當她行走　　　　　　在花園　　　　　她聞到味道

something wet.

某樣東西濕濕的

⇨ 她走在花園時聞到潮溼的味道。

一篇文章，要分成幾個有意義的詞組？

可放入（／）符號來區隔有意義詞組的地方，一般是在（1）「主詞＋動詞」之後；（2）and 和 but 等連接詞之前；（3）that、who 等關係代名詞之前；（4）副詞子句的前後，會用（／）符號來區隔。初學者可能在一篇文章中畫很多（／）符號，但隨著閱讀實力的提升，（／）會減少。時間一久，在不太複雜的文章中即使不畫（／）符號，也能一眼就理解整句的意義。

使用（／）符號來閱讀理解英語篇章
1. 能熟悉英文的句型和構造。
2. 可加速閱讀速度。

該方法對於需要邊聽理解的英文聽力也有很好的效果。
從現在開始，早日丟棄過去理解文章的習慣吧！

以直接閱讀理解的方式，重新閱讀《唐吉訶德》

　　從原文中摘錄一小段。以具有意義的詞組將文章做斷句區分，重新閱讀並做理解練習。

He knew / that she told a lie / at the party.
他知道　／她說了一個謊　　　／在那個派對上。

In the Spanish village of La Mancha, / there lived a gentleman/
在西班牙的鄉村拉曼查，　　　　　　／住著一位紳士　　　　　　／

who loved to read.//
他喜愛閱讀。//

His favorite stories were / of knights and their code of chivalry: /
他最熱愛的故事是　　　　／騎士與騎士精神　　　　　　　　　／

full of dragons, magic swords, enchanted forests, and damsels in distress. //
充滿龍、魔劍、魔法森林以及遇難少女的故事。//

This gentleman was not a wealthy man, / but rather a hidalgo.//
這位紳士並非有錢人　　　　　　　　　/ 而是個西班牙的紳士。//

A hidalgo was a landowner / who was richer than a peasant, /
西班牙紳士是個地主　　　　/ 比農夫有錢　　　　　　　　　/

but poorer than a nobleman. //
比貴族貧窮。//

His name was Senor Quixano. //
他的名字叫做吉哈納先生。//

Senor Quixano lived modestly / with his housekeeper and his young niece.//
吉哈納先生安逸地生活　　　/ 與女管家和姪女同住。//

He was a tall, thin man / in his fifties. //
這位先生高而清瘦　　　/ 五十多歲。//

He was a strong and healthy man, / who went hunting every morning.//
他身強體壯　　　　　　　　　/ 每天早上都喜歡去打獵。//

However, / he started to read adventure stories / all the time. //
然而　　/ 他卻開始閱讀騎士小說　　　　　　　/ 所有的時間。//

His best friends, the local priest and the village barber, / were worried.//
他最好的朋友，當地的牧師和理髮師　　　　　　　　　　/ 很擔心。//

Their friend suddenly began spending night and day / in his chair, /
他們的這位朋友突然開始沒日沒夜地　　　　　　　　　/ 在椅子上 /

reading adventure books / through crazed, bloodshot eyes. //
閱讀騎士小說　　　　　/ 用那瘋狂而布滿血絲的雙眼。//

Soon he started thinking / these stories were true. //
不久他開始認為　　　　/ 這些故事都是真的。//

Finally / he went completely crazy.//
最後　　/ 他幾乎已經走火入魔了。//

Waking up in his reading chair one morning, /
某日早晨從閱讀椅上醒來，/

Senor Quixano announced, / "I'm going to become a knight-errant!"//
吉哈納先生宣布：　　　　/「我要成為一名遊俠騎士。」//

"A what?" / asked his concerned niece. //
「一名什麼？」/ 他憂心忡忡的姪女問道。//

"A knight-errant is a righter of wrongs, / a friend to the unfortunate, /
「遊俠騎士是錯誤的改正者　　　/ 倒楣人的朋友 /

a rescuer of fair maidens, / and a killer of dragons!"//
美女的救星　　　　/ 以及龍的剋星！」//

"But Uncle," /she cried, / "there are no dragons in Spain! //
「但是叔叔，」/ 她喊道/「西班牙沒有龍！//

And who are these maidens / who need rescuing?" //
而且誰又是這些少女　　　/ 需要幫助？」//

The old man went to the attic of his house /
這個男人跑到他的閣樓　　　　　　/

and found a rusty old suit of armor. //
找到一套生鏽的盔甲。//

He put the suit on / and felt ready for action.//
他穿上它　　/ 並準備行動。//

In a bold voice, / he announced, / "Now, to my faithful steed!" //
以厚實的聲音　/ 他宣布　　　/「就是此刻，我忠實的坐騎！」//

2 Guide to Listening Comprehension

 When listening to the story, use some of the techniques shown below. If you take time to study some phonetic characteristics of English, listening will be easier.

Get in the flow of English.

English creates a rhythm formed by combinations of strong and weak stress intonations. Each word has its particular stress that combines with other words to form the overall pattern of stress or rhythm in a particular sentence.

When you are speaking and listening to English, it is essential to get in the flow of the rhythm of English. It takes a lot of practice to get used to such a rhythm. So, you need to start by identifying the stressed syllable in a word.

Listen for the strongly stressed words and phrases.

In English, key words and phrases that are essential to the meaning of a sentence are stressed louder. Therefore, pay attention to the words stressed with a higher pitch. When listening to an English recording for the first time, what matters most is to listen for a general understanding of what you hear. Do not try to hear every single word. Most of the unstressed words are articles or auxiliary verbs, which don't play an important role in the general context. At this level, you can ignore them.

Pay attention to liaisons.

In reading English, words are written with a space between them. There isn't such an obvious guide when it comes to listening to English. In oral English, there are many cases when the sounds of words are linked with adjacent words.

For instance, let's think about the phrase "**take off**," which can be used in "take off your clothes." "Take off your clothes" doesn't sound like [teɪk ɔːf] with each of the words completely and clearly separated from the others. Instead, it sounds as if almost all the words in context are slurred together, [ˈteɪkɔːf], for a more natural sound.

Shadow the voice of the native speaker.

Finally, you need to mimic the voice of the native speaker. Once you are sure you know how to pronounce all the words in a sentence, try to repeat them like an echo. Listen to the book again, but this time you should try a fun exercise while listening to the English.

This exercise is called "shadowing." The word "shadow" means a dark shade that is formed on a surface. When used as a verb, the word refers to the action of following someone or something like a shadow. In this exercise, pretend you are a parrot and try to shadow the voice of the native speaker.

Try to mimic the reader's voice by speaking at the same speed, with the same strong and weak stresses on words, and pausing or stopping at the same points.

Experts have already proven this technique to be effective. If you practice this shadowing exercise, your English speaking and listening skills will improve by leaps and bounds. While shadowing the native speaker, don't forget to pay attention to the meaning of each phrase and sentence.

Listen to what you want to shadow many times. Start out by just trying to shadow a few words or a sentence.

 Mimic the CD out loud. You can shadow everything the speaker says as if you are singing a round, or you also can speak simultaneously with the recorded voice of the native speaker.

 As you practice more, try to shadow more. For instance, shadow a whole sentence or paragraph instead of just a few words.

3 Listening Guide

Chapter One page 14–15

In the Spanish village of La Mancha, there (❶) ( ) gentleman who loved to read. His favorite stories were of knights and their code of chivalry: full of dragons, magic swords, enchanted forests, and damsels in distress.

This gentleman was not a wealthy man, but rather a hidalgo. A hidalgo was a landowner who was richer than a peasant, but poorer than a nobleman. His name was Senor Quixano.

Senor Quixano lived modestly with his housekeeper and his young niece. He was a tall, thin man in his fifties. He was a strong and healthy man, who (❷)( ) every morning.

However, he started to read adventure stories all the time. His (❸)( ), the local priest and the village barber, were worried. Their friend suddenly began spending (❹)( )( ) in his chair, reading adventure books through crazed, bloodshot eyes.

Soon he started thinking these stories were true. Finally he went (❺) crazy.

以下為《唐吉訶德》各章節的前半部。一開始若能聽清楚發音，之後就沒有聽力的負擔。先聽過摘錄的章節，之後再反覆聆聽括弧內單字的發音，並仔細閱讀各種發音的說明。以下都是以英語的典型發音為基礎，所做的簡易說明，即使這裡未提到的發音，也可以配合音檔反覆聆聽，如此一來聽力必能更上一層樓。

① **lived a**：lived 與 a 中的 d 連音，唸成 [ˋlɪvdə]。

② **went hunting**：went 中的 t 位於 n 和 h 之間，屬於音節末尾，因此發音變得較輕微，唸起來會像 wenhunting。如同 went out 中 went 的 t 屬於音節末尾，因此唸起來會像 wenout。

③ **best friends**：當 st 是在字尾連接在一起時，因為兩個字母都是吐氣音，故讀音多半只聽得到 s，t 要停在舌間。st 後接 f，讀音很像 besfriends。just 和 last 都是以 st 結尾，所以多半只聽得到 s。

④ **night and day**：and 字尾為 d 且 day 的字首也為 d，因此 and 字尾的 d 不發音，和 day 連在一起，讀音很像 anday。

⑤ **completely**：當音標遇到有 [tl] 或 [tn] 連在一起發音時，t 的音都會輕輕滑過。

Waking up in his reading chair one morning, Senor Quixano (❶), "I'm going to become a knight-errant!"

"A what?" (❷) his concerned niece.

"A knight-errant is a righter of wrongs, a (❸) (   ) the unfortunate, a rescuer of fair maidens, and a killer of dragons!"

"But Uncle," she cried, "there are no dragons in Spain! And who are these maidens who need rescuing?"

The old man went to the (❹) of his house and found a rusty old suit of armor. He put the suit on and felt ready for action.

In a bold voice, he announced, "Now, to my faithful (❺)!"

This "steed" was really a worn-out nag. But to his delusional eyes, it was a valiant war horse.

"I name you Rocinante, Queen of the hacks! And I will call myself. . ."

He (❻)(   )(   )(   ) think of the perfect name. "Don Quixote!"

This is the Spanish equivalent of Sir Thigh-piece.

❶ announced：announce 的尾音為 [s]，因此 announce 加上 d 時，[d] 的發音變成 [t]。

❷ asked：asked 中的 ed 接在無聲子音 k 的後面，因此尾音為 [t]。同樣的情形會出現在 p, t, k, s, b, d, g。

❸ friend to：這兩個字連在一起時，由於 friend 的字尾為 d，而 to 的字首為 t，d 與 t 的發音接近，且 t 是字首，故在讀音時，friend 的 d 要退居幕後，含在口中與 t 混和，聽起來只有 t 的聲音。

❹ attic：attic 中有兩個 t，但只要發一個 [t] 的音就好，因此 attic 的音標為 ['ætɪk]。

❺ steed：steed 中 s 碰到 t 時，t 不發無聲子音 [t]，而是有聲子音 [d]，s 碰到 p, t, k 這三個字母時，發音都會有所變化。

❻ took a moment to：took a 一起唸；moment to 一起唸。took a 中的 k 和 a 連音唸成 [kə]，而 moment to 中，moment 字尾與 to 字首皆為 t，因此兩者連在一起發音，因此 to 聽起來像 [t]。

4

Listening Comprehension

 A Listen to the MP3. Write down the sentences and names.

① _____(   )

② _____(   )

③ _____

   (   )

④ _____(   )

B Listen to the MP3. Write down the questions and choose the correct answers.

① _____?

   (a) A brave knight who goes questing once a year

   (b) A landowner who was richer than a peasant

   (c) An evil wizard who changes people's faces

② _____?

   (a) He thought it was a magic hat.

   (b) He thought it was a barber's basin.

   (c) He thought it was a golden battle helmet.

C Listen and fill in the blanks.

(50)

❶ His favorite stories were of knights and their
_____ of _____ .

❷ Don Quixote made everyone think he had
_____ his _____ .

❸ Don Quixote _____ himself in the
_____ with a large rock.

❹ Sancho _____ and _____ his
donkey in the group's direction.

❺ Sancho pulled out his _____ and
_____ it in two.

D Listen, dictate what you hear and mark "T" if true or "F" if false.

(51)

T F **❶** _____

T F **❷** _____

T F **❸** _____

T F **❹** _____

T F **❺** _____

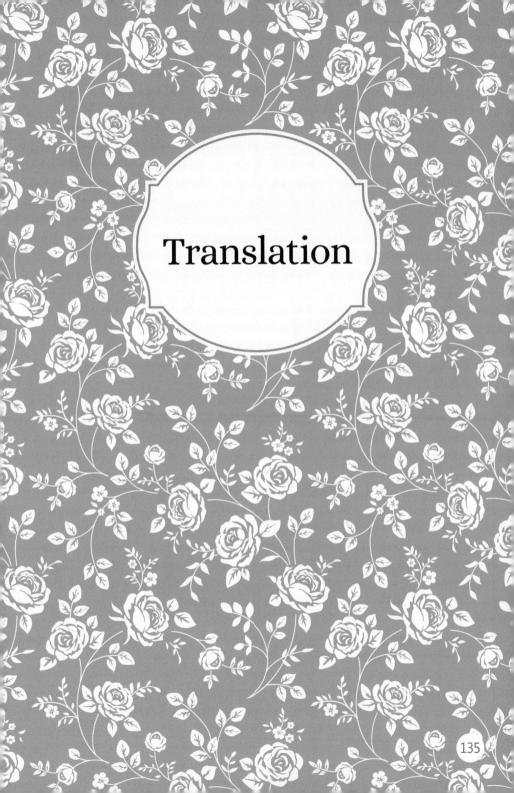

Translation

米格爾・德・塞萬提斯
（Miguel de Cervantes Saavedra, 1547–1616）

　　米格爾・德・塞萬提斯是個西班牙詩人、小說家與劇作家。他生於鄰近馬德里的埃納雷斯堡，是家中第四個孩子，家境貧寒，無法受正規學校教育。

　　1569 年他前往義大利為紅衣主教工作，隔年加入軍隊，度過 5 年軍旅生活。1575 年返回西班牙途中，他受巴巴里海盜俘虜，並被販售為奴，成為阿爾及爾總督的財產。雖然 1580 年他被雙親與修道士贖身，回到西班牙，但生命仍然崎嶇。他成為作家、採購員、稅吏，但仕途不順，還兩次因銀行帳戶異常入獄。

　　1605 年，終於因傑作《唐吉訶德》第一部的出版而迎來巨大成功。此書雖沒替他掙來大筆財富，卻贏來文人的名聲。其後他出版許多小說與劇本，1615 年出版《唐吉訶德》第二部。

　　儘管寫作上獲得成功，他卻沒有足夠的錢過舒適的生活。第二部出版的隔年，1616 年 4 月 23 日他於馬德里去世，享壽 69 歲。儘管生命考驗重重，塞萬提斯終其一生態度正面，心靈健全。

《唐吉訶德》的全名為《來自曼查的紳士唐吉訶德大人》（*The Ingenious Hidalgo Don Quixote of La Mancha*），為經典文學之一，名列有史以來最佳小說，獨特地激發許多文類的出現。故事兩大主角唐吉訶德與扈從桑丘，雖態度與個性彼此衝突，但不分年齡國籍廣受讀者愛戴。

年紀 50 有餘的阿隆索·吉哈納，居住在西班牙拉曼查。因過度沈迷英勇遊歷的騎士故事，而陷入老邁糊塗、意識不清的狀態，他深信自己是個名為「唐吉訶德」的騎士。為了得到頭銜，他與老瘦馬羅西南多啟程冒險。

在遭受羞辱、與被托利多的商人毆打後，唐吉訶德回到家鄉。隨後，他成功說服扈從桑丘·潘薩和他踏上一場新的旅程，兩人便在清晨偷偷地離開。從那之後，他們滑稽的冒險展開，充滿著詼諧與幽默……

p. 12-13

Don Quixote 唐吉訶德

我本來叫做阿隆索‧吉哈納，但我為自己取名為「唐吉訶德」。在困難重重的冒險中，我也以「愁眉苦臉的騎士」為人所知，這是扈從幫我取的名字。然而，每個偉大的騎士都會遭逢困難，但絕不會放棄，因為那樣很可恥。

Sancho Panza 桑丘‧潘薩

在成為主人的扈從之前，我是一位農夫。主人向我保證，我們的這趟冒險會使我致富。不過我開始在想主人的神智是否正常，因為他攻擊了羊群和風車。我試著告訴他那只是羊群和風車而已，但他卻認為對方是敵軍和邪惡的巨人。

Priest and Barber 牧師和理髮師

我們是唐吉訶德的朋友，我們最近開始很擔心他。他以前是位正常的地主，之後卻變得瘋狂，而且沈迷於閱讀冒險故事。我們必須做點事來讓他回歸現實。

Carrasco 卡拉斯科

唐吉訶德的朋友說服我，要我想辦法把唐吉訶德留在家中。如果我假裝是騎士，並向他下戰帖決鬥，那我就可以要他發誓，他要是戰敗了，就要安分地待在家裡。

我們只是很單純地喜愛唐吉訶德，因為他真的很好笑！我們邀請他來城堡享用豐盛的晚宴，很開心地聽他說著那些瘋狂的故事。我們還讓他和他的扈從在我們的庭院裡，矇著眼、騎著假馬。那真的很好笑！

[第一章] 來自拉曼查的男子

p. 14–15　在西班牙的鄉村拉曼查，住著一個愛看書的男人。他最迷騎士和騎士精神之類的故事了，裡面都是在講龍啊、魔劍啊、魔法森林啊，或是落難少女的故事。

這位男子並非富人，而是個西班牙紳士。他只是個比農夫有錢，但比貴族貧窮的地主。他的名字叫做吉哈納先生。

吉哈納先生安逸地與女管家和姪女住在一起。這位先生五十多歲，高高瘦瘦的，身強體壯，他每天早上都會去打獵。

然而，他卻開始將所有時間都花在閱讀騎士小說上。他最好的朋友們，也就是當地的牧師和理髮師，他們都很擔心，因為他們的這位朋友突然開始瘋狂地用布滿血絲的雙眼，沒日沒夜地在椅子上閱讀騎士小說。

不久，他便開始認為這些故事都是真的，他已經走火入魔了。

p. 16–17　某日早晨從閱讀椅上醒來，吉哈納先生宣布了一件事：「我要成為一名遊俠騎士。」

「一名什麼？」他憂心忡忡的姪女問道。

「遊俠騎士是錯誤的改正者、倒楣人的朋友、美女的救星、龍的剋星！」

「叔叔，但是西班牙沒有龍呀！」她喊道：「而且這些需要幫助的少女又是誰？」

這個老男人跑到閣樓，找到一套生鏽的盔甲，穿上它準備行動。

他以渾厚的聲音宣布說：「瞧，這是我忠實的坐騎！」

實際上那「坐騎」只是一匹老老垂矣的老馬，但在他妄想的眼中，那是匹英勇的戰馬。

「我命名你為羅西南多，戰馬之后。而我稱我自己為⋯⋯」

他花了一會兒想了個赫赫大名。「唐吉訶德！」

這個名字在西班牙語中，是「腿庫先生」的意思。

p. 18–19 「現在，我必須把我的生命獻給某位小姐！」

「你有任何意中人嗎？」被男人瘋狂自言自語所驚嚇到的姪女抽噎地問。

「所有騎士都有奉獻的對象，」男人回答：「當我戰勝巨人或是逮到惡棍，我會將他們帶到她的面前誇耀，以證明我的愛與忠誠。」

接著他突然想起了他聽過一位住在鄰近埃爾・托波索村莊的美麗鄉下姑娘。沈湎在幻想中的唐吉訶德，決定把她當作是落難公主。

「她的名字是什麼？」姪女要求他回答，期盼他能回到現實。

不久後，他自己想出了一個名字：「所有漂亮的小姐都叫做杜爾西內雅。那位姑娘的名字就是杜爾西內雅·埃爾·托波索，我會把我的生命奉獻給她。不要阻止我，我得要走了！」

之後唐吉訶德拿起他的劍、破裂的舊長矛和皮盾前往馬廄。幾分鐘後，他騎馬而去，踏上他第一次的騎士冒險之旅。

唐吉訶德不久後意識到自己還沒被封為騎士。「我必須找到貴族或是小姐來為我加冕，」他說道：「我可不想被別人稱作騙子！」

`p. 20–21` 唐吉訶德一整天都在酷熱的草原上尋找冒險，但一無所獲。夕陽西下時，他和羅西南多都又餓又累。在漸漸昏暗的光線下，這個穿著盔甲的男子找到了一間小旅館往前騎去。「也許我們可以在那個城堡找到一個歇腳處。」他對他的馬說著。

這間旅館其實只是西班牙公路旁常見的那種破爛旅社。旅館前站著兩位臉上帶有髒汙的鄉下女孩，她們看到穿著生鏽盔甲男子的到來，感到一陣驚訝。

「晚安，親愛的美人們！」他說著：「我是騎士，名為唐吉訶德·拉曼查。請用喇叭來宣告我的到來。」

在他的眼中，這間小旅館是個有著銀色高塔的壯麗城堡。當這些女孩咯咯地笑著時，唐吉訶德有點惱怒。

然而就在此時，一位豬倌從旅館走出，他吹奏著號角，要趁天黑之前把豬隻聚集起來。唐吉訶德卻誤把號角當成是管樂與喇叭的樂隊奏樂。

p. 22-23 客棧老闆接著走向騎士，說道：「如果您在找住宿的地方，很抱歉這裡已經客滿了。」

「陛下，你是城堡的主人嗎？」唐吉訶德禮貌地問道。

看著這個穿著生鏽盔甲的男人，客棧老闆心想他一定是瘋了，所以決定要來捉弄一下這個鄉巴佬。

「城堡內高貴的客房都被住滿了。」他說道。

唐吉訶德回答：「沒關係，優秀的騎士不需要住得舒適，我很樂意以石為枕、睡在地板上。」

「你真的是個騎士，對吧？」老闆促狹地問道。

「我是個見習騎士，」唐吉訶德回答：「我在找一位能用劍為我加冕的貴族。」

老闆說道：「我了解了，但我現在忙著招待其他客人。如果有機會的話，我會回來為你加冕。」

「非常感謝您，我的主人。」唐吉訶德答道。

p. 24-25 在小憩一會兒後，唐吉訶德變得沒有耐性，就派人去找老闆。老闆一到，唐吉訶德就馬上說：「閣下，我沒辦法再等下去了！請告訴我，要怎麼做才能得到騎士的稱號。」

老闆說：「如果想讓我為你加冕，今晚就留在這裡幫我守衛庭院。」

唐吉訶德一聽，就轉身踏步走向廚房。

他拿起武器，走到飲水槽旁的庭院中央。在旅館裡頭的老闆告訴客人說，有個瘋狂的男子認為自己是庭院裡的騎士。

幾小時之後，一個騾夫帶著牲畜來到飲水槽。

「退後，你這個愚笨的騎士！」唐吉訶德大叫：「我要誓死保衛這口魔井。」

「可是我的騾子要喝水啊。」鄉人推開唐吉訶德喊道。

唐吉訶德擺動長矛，攻擊男子的頭部，把他擊昏了。

「我已經做了第一件英勇事蹟！」唐吉訶德喊道：「當這個人醒來，我要把他送到杜爾西內雅小姐面前，要他向她致意。」

p. 26-27 打架的聲音吵到了其他的騾夫，他們衝進旅館，攻擊唐吉訶德。

「有一群邪惡的騎士攻擊我！」唐吉訶德用自己的盾牌阻擋對方襲來的飛石喊道。

此時老闆才驚覺，自己應該要擺脫這個危險的怪人。

他向唐吉訶德說道：「親愛的騎士，寬恕這些邪惡的騎士並放下你的武器！你已經向我證明了你的勇氣，現在我會馬上為你加冕，請單膝跪地。」

唐吉訶德順從地跪在院子的稻草和牛糞之中。

「我藉此任命你為正義騎士階級。」老闆用自己的劍在唐吉訶德的背上輕輕一拍並大喊。

唐吉訶德興奮地一躍而起，說道：「閣下，我會絕對服從您！」

「是的，是的！」老闆答道：「現在你必須去執行善行、糾正惡行。」

「我馬上就出發！」唐吉訶德大叫，迫不及待前往馬廄、騎上羅西南多，奔向日暮黃昏的拉曼查。

p. 28~29 不久之後，唐吉訶德在路上發現一群迎面而來的絲綢商人。

「這是個表現英勇行為的好機會。」

他騎到隊伍前，阻擋他們的去路，說道：「停下來，你們這群笨蛋！如果不承認我親愛的杜爾西內雅·埃爾·托波索是世界上最美麗的女人，誰都休想通過！」

這群商人停了下來，看了看彼此，他們意識到面前這個人很顯然是個瘋子。

「在我承認她的美貌之前，我想先一睹芳澤。我們怎麼知道她會不會只是個又老又肥的女人呢？」商人中一個愛說笑的人講道。

「又老又肥的女人？」唐吉訶德生氣地大叫：「準備受死吧，你們這群無禮的惡棍！」唐吉訶德抓起長矛向那些人猛然刺去，但羅西南多不堪疾速，摔倒在地。唐吉訶德也隨之被拋向空中，碰地一聲摔到溝裡。商人們大聲地嘲笑他後，繼續趕路。

幾個小時以後，一位路過的農夫聽見啜泣聲，發現跌坐在溝裡、滿身灰塵的唐吉訶德。農夫認出他是從村莊來的吉哈納先生，所以趕緊把他救出來，帶回唐吉訶德的家中。唐吉訶德就在自己的床上安穩地抱膝而睡。

[第二章] 騎士與扈從

p. 32~33 兩個禮拜以來唐吉訶德都在自己的家裡休息，這讓每個人都以為他恢復了正常。但其實他已經偷偷把一些土地賣掉，用來當做下次冒險的盤纏，此外他也在尋找一位可以結伴同行的扈從。

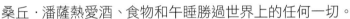

　　唐吉訶德唯一找到可以為他工作的人，是一位胖胖的農夫，他叫做桑丘·潘薩，是個不折不扣的傻瓜。

　　「扈從的工作聽起來好困難喔！」桑丘說道：「我還是寧願跟家人在一起，大口咀嚼一整盤的豬肉好了。」

　　桑丘·潘薩熱愛酒、食物和午睡勝過世界上的任何一切。

　　「但是，扈從都可以從服侍的騎士那裡得到大把的黃金和土地作為獎賞。」唐吉訶德向他承諾：「如果你願意服侍我，你最後一定會成為某個富裕島嶼的總督。」

　　「我自己的島嶼！」桑丘舔了一下他的嘴唇說道：「那好，我會帶上我的行囊，並且為我的驢子套上馬鞍。」

　　接著，這兩個人在午夜時悄悄地離開了。

　　p. 34–35 破曉時，這兩個男人站在一片遼闊的平原中間。當唐吉訶德斜眼瞥見刺眼明亮的太陽時，他看到眼前的平原上有三、四十座風車。

　　「桑丘，幸運之神正對著我們微笑呢！」他大聲說。

　　「這表示要吃早餐了嗎？」桑丘回答。

　　「現在根本無暇吃東西，你這豬頭！看看在那裡的巨人，我會把他們都一一殺掉，我們偉大的功績將會流傳於世！」

　　「什麼巨人啊？」桑丘大叫。

　　「就在那裡啊！有著長長手臂的那些巨人！」

　　「可是主人，那些是風車啊！」

　　「別反駁我，」唐吉訶德責罵他：「我看見他們時，我就知道他們是一群巨人了！」

唐吉訶德騎著羅西南多向前奔馳而去，並舉起他的長矛。

「巨人們！準備戰鬥吧！」他大聲疾呼。

唐吉訶德向最近的塔樓進攻，將長矛刺向風車翼。他的武器被輾碎，這個武士從馬背上被舉了起來，拋向空中。

唐吉訶德重重地摔到在五十公尺遠的地方，「蹦！」的一聲，揚起了好大一團白色塵煙。

p. 36–37 桑丘加快他的毛驢並說道：「我早告訴你，它們是風車。」

唐吉訶德接著說：「你這個笨蛋！當我衝向這些巨人時，一個邪惡的巫師騎著一匹隱形的馬飛向空中，並施咒使巨人變成風車！他是為了要盜取我的榮耀！」

桑丘回答：「我懂了。」他幫忙把主人扶起來，而且相信了主人所說的每句話。

「別擔心，我的隨從。我會找出這名巫師並擊敗他的！」

隔天早晨，他們未進食就又開始展開冒險之旅，這讓桑丘很沮喪。一個小時後，遠處出現了一大片灰雲。

「這想必是兩支嗜殺成性的軍隊在戰鬥！」唐吉訶德大聲說著。之後他很快地描述了自己編造出來的兩支軍隊的將軍和凶猛騎士們的名字。

「我們要怎麼知道這些不是那個邪惡巫師變出來的戲法？」

「你沒有聽到那數以千計的行軍腳步聲嗎？」唐吉訶德大喊，他把自己破爛的長矛猛然刺向他們。

「他們不是士兵，」桑丘接著大聲說：「那只是一大群羊而已！」

p. 38–39　唐吉訶德開始用長矛串起可憐的羊兒。牧羊人一看到他殺了他們的牲畜，就向唐吉訶德投擲石頭。一顆石頭擊中了唐吉訶德的臉頰，使他從羅西南多上跌了下來。

「這些邪惡的巫師！」唐吉訶德吐出了整口的鮮血和牙齒的碎片，並說道：「我們又中計了！」

騎士和他的扈從在附近的草地上找了夜晚可以歇息的地方。

「我會在一分鐘內準備好晚餐的。」桑丘說道。

「噢，桑丘，在我最沮喪絕望的這一刻，你怎麼還有心情想吃的呢？」

「對我來說，沒有什麼比吃更重要的了。」桑丘吃著生洋蔥和薩拉米香腸說道：「你到底在難過什麼啊？」

唐吉訶德抱著抽痛的頭回答：「我損失了半個耳朵和四顆牙齒，這讓我很難過。」

「我一點也不覺得奇怪。一到兩個禮拜後，你全身上下可能什麼都沒剩了。我沒有見過像你這麼悽慘的人，我們應該要稱呼你為『愁眉苦臉的騎士』，你的下巴好像快要碰到地面了。」

「是的，我的扈從。對一個像我這樣鬱鬱寡歡的騎士來說，這樣的名字再適合不過了。」

p. 40–41　兩人意識到自己口渴了，一個小時後，他們在森林中發現一條小河。太陽慢慢西下，他們聽見森林深處傳來可怕的怪聲。

「這一定是可怕食人惡魔所掌管的魔法森林，我會找出他，用我的雷電長矛擊敗他。如果我在三天內沒有回來，請前去找我的杜爾西內雅小姐，告訴她，我是以她的名義英勇殉身的。」

　　桑丘‧潘薩很害怕落單，所以他滑下驢子，溜到羅西南多的後肢，然後用一圈繩子將牠綁住不動。

　　唐吉訶德鞭策他的老馬，可是老馬動也不動。

　　「這是什麼魔法啊？」唐吉訶德低沈地說：「我的坐騎居然無法移動。」

　　「噢，這一定又是那個邪惡的巫師幹的，」桑丘撒了謊：「也許明天早上再來對付食人惡魔比較好。」

　　「好，我會在早上打破這個魔咒。」唐吉訶德對桑丘的想法表示同意。

p. 42–43 兩人害怕河流下游的恐怖聲音，在夜裡的森林中不斷地發抖。

　　黎明時，桑丘將羅西南多後肢的繩子解開。當唐吉訶德騎上馬時，牠又能動了。

　　「我自由囉！」唐吉訶德高興地說著。接著便出發前去尋找食人惡魔。

　　然而，當他們找到恐怖低沈聲的源頭時，卻發現那不是食人惡魔，而是一台老舊機器，被瀑布的水沖得噹啷作響。

　　桑丘‧潘薩對唐吉訶德這個最新的愚蠢想法大笑了起來。「我們整晚發抖，就是因為害怕這個！」他大笑著說。

　　「愁眉苦臉的騎士」因為這趟失敗的冒險，變得更加痛苦。但是在當天下午，他發現了能夠提振精神的事情。

「你看，桑丘，你有看到朝我們這個方向騎過來的騎士嗎？」

「我看到一個男人騎著一頭驢子。」桑丘回答。

「那位騎士是勇敢的霍勒斯，他的頭盔是世界上最值錢的東西了。」

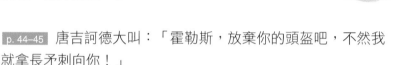

「我想在他頭上的應該是一個理髮師的銅盆吧！」

「不，那是個純金戰鬥頭盔。我要向他挑戰，贏得頭盔！」

p. 44-45 唐吉訶德大叫：「霍勒斯，放棄你的頭盔吧，不然我就拿長矛刺向你！」

「我沒有頭盔。」那個男人喊說：「我只是個理髮師，這個銅盆是工作用的，我會戴在頭上是因為下雨了。」

「你以為我會相信你嗎？」唐吉訶德譏諷他，並拔出長矛。

唐吉訶德從男人身上奪走銅盆，往自己的頭上蓋下去。「頭盔面甲已經不見了，有人想把黃金熔掉，但我會以驕傲的心戴著它。」

桑丘努力忍住不去嘲笑唐吉訶德把銅盆戴在頭上的模樣。

不久，他們遇到了十二個排成一列的男人，他們的脖子和手上都戴著重重的鍊條。有四個士兵監視著他們，士兵們一邊咒罵，一邊用鞭子抽打犯人。

桑丘說著：「那些是犯人，要去當國王的划船夫。」

「我不信！」唐吉訶德接著説：「這些不幸的人們被迫當俘虜，解救他們是我的責任。」

桑丘以警告的口語説：「主人，這些是可怕的罪犯，他們必須為自己的罪行付出代價！」

p. 46–47 「站到一邊去！」其中一個士兵命令著。

「這些人脆弱又貧困，」唐吉訶德説道：「身為一名遊俠騎士，我會保護他們！」

「這個發神經的老笨蛋精神不正常！」士兵大笑地説著：「他把銅盆戴在頭上耶！」

其他士兵也跟著大笑，唐吉訶德用長矛攻擊了士兵的頭，把他給擊昏。其他士兵想攻擊唐吉訶德，他們反先被囚犯襲擊。其中一個犯人偷走士兵袋中的鑰匙，解放了其他犯人。這些犯人輕而易舉地就把士兵們給擊潰了。

「我親愛的朋友們，我已經讓你們自由了。」唐吉訶德大喊：「我只要求你們前往埃爾·托波索，向我的女主人證實我的勇氣。」

「他真是個秀逗的瘋子！」其中一個犯人叫道：「把他抓住！」

犯人們把唐吉訶德和桑丘·潘薩打得頭破血流，並且搶走了鞍囊。他們還在跑走之前，將唐吉訶德頭上的銅盆用石頭砸裂。

桑丘·潘薩哭著説：「現在我們要倒大楣了，我們現在變通緝犯了！聖友團要來追捕我們了！」

p. 50–51 **騎士精神的興衰**

　　騎士精神的概念與中古世紀興起的騎士息息相關。騎士憑藉厚重的盔甲、長矛和長劍，成為戰場上最令人生畏的戰士。

　　有些學者主張，騎士精神的演變來自於日耳曼部落，當時最勇敢的戰士會被揀選為國王的隨侍和護衛。然而，這些早期的日耳曼騎士並不認為保護弱者是騎士精神的主要信念。

　　騎士精神直到 11 世紀才建立：「不說假話、鋤強扶弱、不畏敵」，這樣的行為準則快速地傳遍了整個歐洲。

　　這種浪漫的想法為當時的女性所吸引，由於當時女性被視為是「較弱的性別」，因此騎士會發誓保護她們免於危險。以上的信念演變成，一位英勇強壯的隨侍，就應該要歷經重重的艱鉅任務，來贏得美人心。

　　然而，隨著作戰策略的改變和新發明的出現，騎士的影響不再。騎士的影響力衰退，騎士精神的概念也隨之沒落。

　　文學曾經一度大力吹捧騎士精神，而今卻對它的沒落加以嘲笑。最明顯的例子就是塞萬提斯的小說《唐吉訶德》，騎士精神只存在於紳士行為的浪漫理想。最後，當女性開始維護她們的平等權，並要求男人對她們一視同仁，作者們普遍都認為「騎士精神已死」。

[第三章] 巨人殺手

p. 52–53 為躲避聖友團的追捕，唐吉訶德和桑丘‧潘薩逃到了山上。他們來到了莫雷納山區的一處荒僻之地。

　　「在信念為人所質疑時，每個偉大的人物都會經歷一段沮喪期。」唐吉訶德轉向他那飢餓不已的扈從繼續說道：「我要把你送去埃爾‧托波索，你要帶口信給我的愛人杜爾西內雅。她得告訴我，是否要回報我的心意。我會留在這裡鞭打我自己，直到你回來為止。」

　　桑丘一心一意只想著，當他回到鄉村時，就能大啖美食啦。

　　「騎快一點，桑丘‧潘薩。」唐吉訶德以命令的口吻說著，並脫下他的盔甲。接著他用大塊的石頭猛撞自己的胸口，並用樹枝抽打自己的背部。

　　桑丘離去時看到此景，便大聲地對他的主人說：「不要做得太過火了，不然等我回來時，你可能就死無全屍了。」

p. 54–55 在走回村子的半路上，桑丘停在一間客棧享用他期待已久的大餐。當他吃飽喝足準備離開時，碰見了唐吉訶德的老朋友們——牧師和理髮師。

　　「嘿，你替我們那位有問題的朋友吉哈納先生工作，對吧？」牧師向桑丘問道。

　　「沒錯，我是他的扈從。」

　　「你怎麼會聽信他的胡言亂語呢？難道你沒有發現他已經失去理智了嗎？」

　　「的確是有些奇怪的事情發生。」桑丘答道。

　　「他現在人在哪裡呢？」理髮師急切地想知道。

　　「他在山上等著我帶他的愛人杜爾西內雅‧埃爾‧托波索女士的答覆回去。」

　　「她的什麼答覆？」牧師問道。

　　「就愛情的事啦。」桑丘回答。

　　「帶我們去找他，我們要把他帶回村子。」牧師說道。

「好啊，不過我先警告你們，他不會那麼輕易跟你們回去的。」

理髮師接著說：「嗯，我有個計畫，等我一下。」

不久以後，理髮師帶了兩套客棧老闆娘的洋裝回來。

p. 56–57 這三個男人往山上走去，當晚他們在那裡紮營，並討論計畫的細節。一早，桑丘便回去找唐吉訶德，並告訴他有女子們需要幫助。就在同時，牧師和理髮師著裝完畢，接著在火上烹煮培根當作早餐。當他們邊吃邊聊時，看見一位美麗的女子經過此地。

「我們應該要馬上向她自我介紹才對。」牧師說道，接著他們跑到了女子面前。

當她看見他們時，嚇得尖叫想逃跑。

「孩子，別怕。」牧師大叫：「我是上帝的使者。」

「如果你是牧師，為什麼要穿成這副德性呢？」她問道。

「一言難盡啊！」他答道。

「那麼，妳怎麼會在這山區裡遊蕩？」理髮師問道。

這個美麗的女子於是把她悲慘的故事告訴了他們。

「我的名字是多羅泰雅。我是一位富裕農民的女兒。我本來要和公爵的兒子費迪南多結婚，但他拋下我，和另一個女人在一起。這讓我痛徹心扉，所以決定在這裡以淚洗面，度過餘生。」

p. 58–59 此時牧師腦中冒出一個想法，「也許像妳這樣真正美麗的小姐，可以說服唐吉訶德回到我們的村子，而不是由我們這兩個老牧師和理髮師來扮成女人。」

多羅泰雅同意他們的計畫,並穿上其中一件洋裝。

桑丘回來時,便帶他們去找唐吉訶德,此時唐吉訶德仍在用橄欖樹的樹枝鞭打自己。

多羅泰雅立刻跪了下來說:「勇敢的騎士,求求你,一位可怕的巨人正在攻擊我父親的王國,請你救救我們!」

「沒有問題,我一定會幫助你們!桑丘,備馬。我們要馬上離開,我無法拒絕受難公主的要求。」

之後,他們一行人抵達了桑丘和牧師、理髮師第一次相遇的小旅館。旅館老闆向前去迎接他們,並私底下與牧師見面。牧師遞給老闆十個金幣並告訴他說:「我那穿著銀色盔甲的朋友瘋了,他以為自己是騎士,還把這裡當成城堡。我請你今晚配合一下,讓我們待到明天早上。」

p. 60-61 「是啊,我老婆聽說有個精神錯亂的人在山谷裡遊蕩。」老闆接著說:「我也知道聖友團在追捕他。你們可以留在裡頭,不過你那位秀逗的朋友必須待在我藏酒的秣草棚,確保他不會亂來。」

牧師和理髮師都同意老闆的想法。

午夜已過,當每個人都已進入夢鄉時,牧師卻被湧出的水聲所吵醒,感覺彷彿是河水突然沖進了小旅館。這時桑丘‧潘薩突然全身血跡斑斑地跌進房裡。「我的主人正在樓上和巨人戰鬥!那裡正在上演一場大屠殺!」

牧師把桑丘扶起來，嚐了一下他手指上的紅色液體。「桑丘，這不是血，你這傻瓜，這是葡萄酒！」

牧師趕緊跑上樓，卻被眼前所發生的事情給嚇到。唐吉訶德正揮舞他的劍，捅向吊在天花板上那個裝滿紅葡萄酒的酒囊。

「啊哈！」當酒潑在唐吉訶德身上使他眼花撩亂時，他大喊：「又是一個致命的傷口，不久後你身上的血將會流光，勝利是屬於我的！」

p. 62–63 旅館老闆衝到樓上並大叫：「噢，不，你這個瘋子。我最上等的紅葡萄酒都流光了，我老婆已經去找聖友團了，你要為我的損害付出代價！」

聖友團的警察抵達並逮捕了唐吉訶德，牧師向前去把其中一個警察帶至旁邊一會兒。他解釋說，唐吉訶德已經瘋了，需要送回家做醫藥治療，牧師還請警察們在自己的臉上撲些粉。

不久，多羅泰雅走向唐吉訶德說：「勇敢的騎士，你已經殺死巨人，拯救了我父親的王國，我衷心感謝你。」

「這是我的榮幸，親愛的公主。」唐吉訶德說道。

突然間，騎士被八個白臉狀似鬼魅的形體所包圍。

其中一個人走向前說道：「我們是邪惡巫師派來的魔鬼，要帶你回你的村子！乖乖地進入這個籠子裡吧！」

唐吉訶德想抵抗，但那八個男人將他抓住，把他鎖進籠子裡。唐吉訶德不斷掙扎想逃離籠子，直到氣力殆盡後就昏了過去。

[第四章] 嶄新的探索

p. 66–67 唐吉訶德在床上躺了幾個星期，他的姪女和女管家都在床邊悉心照顧他，期盼他的騎士狂想曲就此結束。

有一天，理髮師和牧師來拜訪他。

「我已經完全康復了，準備好回到原本正常的生活。」唐吉訶德説道。

「那麼，老友啊！」牧師接著問道：「你覺得針對土耳其蘇丹進犯我們的國家，國王應該怎麼做才好？」

「我會舉辦一個騎馬比武的競賽，找出全西班牙最勇敢的武士，然後我會送這位英勇的騎士去征服蘇丹敵軍。」唐吉訶德説。

唐吉訶德起身下床，示範了如何用劍擊敗蘇丹的軍隊。

理髮師對著牧師説道：「噢，天啊，看來我們這位老朋友的神智尚未清醒。我們應該要使用更震撼的手段，來使他恢復正常。」

桑丘突然面露微笑地跑進房間，告訴這位老騎士一些好消息。

p. 68–69 「昨晚我去參加一個迎接年輕卡拉斯科歸鄉的派對，他在薩拉曼卡大學唸書。我還沒來得及跟他打招呼，他就對我説，他讀了我們所有的冒險故事。」桑丘繼續説道：「有人寫了一本名為《唐吉訶德》的書，這本書成了全西班牙最佳的暢銷書！」

「帶他來見我，我的扈從，我要見見這位年輕人。」唐吉訶德説道。

幾分鐘後，桑丘帶著一位肥肥胖胖、面帶逗趣表情的年輕人進到房間裡來。唐吉訶德尚未開口前，這位年輕人跪下來說道：「噢！偉大的騎士，能見到您真是我的榮幸！」

卡拉斯科滔滔不絕地繼續說下去，盡力忍住不笑。「在騎士的歷史中，再也找不到比唐吉訶德更勇敢不凡的騎士了。這本書受到社會上各階級的人們深深喜愛，作者甚至談到要寫續集呢！」

唐吉訶德跳下床並說：「非常好，該是回到馬鞍上的時候了，我的觀眾需要我！」

p. 70–71 七天之後，唐吉訶德和桑丘‧潘薩為馬匹備鞍，準備踏上旅程。卡拉斯科在那裡向他們道別。

突然間女管家和姪女衝出房子喊道：「這裡發生了什麼事？牧師在哪裡？他要阻止這個瘋子啊！」

卡拉斯科小聲對他們說：「別擔心，牧師和我有個計畫能讓他乖乖回家，一兩天後你們就會看到他了。」

接著唐吉訶德向他們道別，然後策馬出發。

「那我們現在要往哪個方向去啊？」騎了一個小時後桑丘問道。

「我們要前往埃爾‧托波索，你要指引我到親愛女主人的王宮。」

桑丘苦惱地說道：「噢，不，我不確定我是否記得她住的地方。」

不久，他們發現自己騎到了埃爾·托波索的黑暗街道，完全迷了路。桑丘說服唐吉訶德，等天亮了再去找杜爾西內雅。他們在野營地吃過早餐後，桑丘離開，想找出之後的辦法。

p. 72–73 桑丘思索著對策，這時他看見平原上來了三位騎著驢子的鄉村姑娘。他靈機一動，就掉頭騎回營地。

「主人，我有重大的消息。」桑丘大喊。

「她允許我去造訪她嗎？」唐吉訶德滿心期盼地問道。

「擦亮你的盔甲，她帶著兩位女僕，往這裡過來了。」

唐吉訶德驚慌失措地到處亂跑。桑丘幫忙他穿上盔甲。幾分鐘後，他們騎到了樹林附近。

「她在哪裡？」唐吉訶德大叫。

「就在那裡啊！」桑丘指著那些騎驢經過的鄉下姑娘說。

「我只看到三個騎著驢子的醜陋女孩。」唐吉訶德說道。

「但是，先生，那些是我看過最漂亮的女人了。」

唐吉訶德走向她們，並向中間的那位女孩問道：「請問妳是杜爾西內雅，西班牙最甜美的玫瑰花嗎？」

那位女孩放聲大笑，說道：「抱歉啊，老爺爺，我不能浪費時間和瘋子講話。」

接著她用力踢了桑丘一下，害他差一點就跌下驢子。女孩們逕自離開，留下陷入愁雲慘霧的唐吉訶德。

p. 74–75 「邪惡的巫師將我的愛人變成了一個醜陋的村姑！」唐吉訶德大叫地說。

「真是太恐怖了。」桑丘大叫，其實他拍手叫好，因為他的計畫成功了。

「現在我真的是個『愁眉苦臉的騎士』了。這個邪惡的巫師重擊我的要害！我一定要找個方法來破除魔咒，恢復她的美貌！」

唐吉訶德接著一直在樹林裡哭泣，朗誦著失戀的詩句。桑丘則大快朵頤地吃了兩個薩拉米香腸，還喝掉一整桶的酒。

唐吉訶德突然小聲地說道：「我聽到有兩個男人接近森林的聲音。」

「哪裡？」桑丘問道。

「在灌木叢的另一邊。」

接著這兩個男人靜靜地仔細地聽。

「我親愛的小姐，卡希爾達，是西班牙最美麗的女人！」那個聲音說道：「她賦予我這個『森林騎士』的任務，就是要除去所有不以為然的騎士。」

「這個騎士在胡扯。」唐吉訶德小聲地說。

p. 76–77 「你們完全錯了！」唐吉訶德走出灌木叢，對著騎士喊道：「我要告訴你，我的杜爾西內雅才是世界上最美麗的女子。」

「看來我們必須一決高下。」另一個騎士冷漠地回答。

「那我們就在黎明時騎馬決鬥吧。」唐吉訶德答道。

「好的，但是有一個條件，輸的一方要回到自己的村子，並且發誓一年內都會待在家鄉，不再參加任何戰鬥。」

「我接受。」唐吉訶德回答。

隔天黎明時，兩位騎士現身在林中空地的兩端。在「森林騎士」左方的是他的扈從，一位有著紫色大鼻子的駝背人士。

「森林騎士」冷不防地加快坐騎，向唐吉訶德的方向奔馳而去，舉起長矛猛攻。唐吉訶德隨即拿起長矛。就在這最後一刻，「森林騎士」的馬嘶吼著，不肯再向前跨出一步。唐吉訶德用盡全身氣力猛然攻擊另一個騎士的馬鞍，他跳下羅西南多，拔出寶劍，按住對方的脖子。

p. 78–79「你投降了嗎？」唐吉訶德問道。

「森林騎士」大叫哭著說：「是的，我戰敗了。」

接著唐吉訶德命令桑丘把騎士的頭盔拿掉。

桑丘大叫：「哎喲，這個騎士看起來像是卡拉斯科！」

「沒錯，看起來的確很像。」唐吉訶德說道：「這個邪惡巫師將人變臉的魔法真是高明。」

「不，我真的是卡拉斯科。」這個學者啜泣地說。

桑丘接著說：「現在把他殺了比較妥當，這樣才可以免除後患。」

唐吉訶德舉起他的劍要攻擊他，但駝背人士突然飛奔而來，並脫下長袍。原來他是唐吉訶德的好友，理髮師。「拿開你的劍。」他說道。

唐吉訶德接著說：「太驚人了，這個邪惡的巫師真是神通廣大。」

理髮師將卡拉斯科拖回營區，大聲罵說唐吉訶德的情況並沒有因為這場決鬥而好轉。

隔天早上，唐吉訶德和桑丘·潘薩騎著馬來到了麥田，戰勝「森林騎士」的感覺，讓唐吉訶德內心澎湃。他絲毫沒有懷疑過那是牧師密謀要帶他回村子所做的計謀。

p. 80–81 騎士和他的扈從走在路上時碰上了皇家的馬車。唐吉訶德舉起長矛，擋住馬車的去路，說道：「停下來，不然我就把你切成兩半。我要知道馬車裡有什麼。」

　　「有一頭獅子，這是非洲王子獻給國王的禮物。」其中一個車夫說。

　　「危險嗎？」唐吉訶德問道。

　　「牠嗜血成性，而且現在又更危險，因為牠餓了。所以老先生，快讓開吧，不然你會受傷的。」

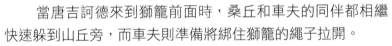

　　「我可是唐吉訶德，」這個騎士大聲宣稱：「我才不怕任何的貓！」

　　接著他將長矛對著車夫的鼻子，說道：「把籠子打開！」

　　當唐吉訶德來到獅籠前面時，桑丘和車夫的同伴都相繼快速躲到山丘旁，而車夫則準備將綁住獅籠的繩子拉開。

　　「你真的不再考慮一下嗎？」車夫問道。

　　「唐吉訶德從來不畏懼任何危險！」騎士大喊：「打開門吧！」

　　籠門喀喀作響地開了，一隻巨大的獅子伸出牠的頭，牠黑色的下巴覆蓋著一層厚厚的口水，黃色的牙齒像彎刀一樣，眼神就像火焰般閃耀著。

p. 82–83 「我等著你，森林之王。」唐吉訶德毫無畏懼地大喊：「你害怕現身在我面前嗎？」

獅子瞪了老騎士一會兒，打個哈欠後就睡著了。

「這隻獅子是個懦夫！」唐吉訶德怒罵：「車夫，晃動牠的籠子，讓牠吼叫！」

「我才不要！」車夫丟下獅籠附近的繩子，答道：「你是西班牙最勇敢的男人，沒有人敢挑戰這個殺人獸。」

「你願意向我們的國王宣誓嗎？」唐吉訶德問道。

「他將會對你的英勇事蹟有最詳細的了解。」車夫回答。

唐吉訶德向桑丘和車夫的同伴作勢，表示現在已安全無虞。

「從今開始，我希望我以『霸獅騎士』而聲名遠播。」唐吉訶德宣告：「這個冒險故事將流傳於世！」

p. 86-87 夢與現實

《唐吉訶德》被視為是史上最傑出的小說之一，這原本是出人意料之外的。塞萬提斯最初只是想寫出一個關於騎士精神的短篇滑稽浪漫故事。作者想藉機嘲弄那些以英勇為名，試圖以擊敗可怕怪獸來贏得美人心的騎士們。

塞萬提斯的英雄——唐吉訶德，是一位精神錯亂、不切實際的人。他穿著粗糙的盔甲，騎著老馬四處闖蕩，顯得荒謬至極。而他的敵人，實則是他在瘋狂想像中所虛構出來的。本書早期的大多數忠實讀者，把這本書視為是塞萬提斯節奏明快的幽默之作。

然而多年以後，大眾徹底翻轉了先前的看法。如果讀者深究故事的主題，就會發現這是一個溫馨且充滿人性的故事，故事的主角在努力實踐他的理想。唐吉訶德這個愚蠢的騎士，被視為是過時浪漫理想主義的象徵，企圖在這個逐漸冷漠現實的世界裡，求得一個生存的空間。

與唐吉訶德的理想主義相異的，是他的扈從桑丘‧潘薩。相較於主人唐吉訶德的幻覺，桑丘象徵著現實。然而桑丘似乎也隨之變得瘋狂，因為他一心想致富，所以跟隨了唐吉訶德的腳步。雖然他能夠辨別唐吉訶德所看到的邪惡巨人實際上是風車，但他和主人一樣愚蠢。這讓讀者開始在思考，究竟在不切實際與過於現實之間，何者比較愚蠢？

[第五章] 最後的冒險

`p. 88–89` 在唐吉訶德帶一行人前往森林的這三天，桑丘一直覺得又悶又氣，因為他們幾乎要斷糧了，我們故事主人翁的扈從，必須挨餓地睡在潮濕的毯子上，一邊擔心受怕，怕野狼等掠食性動物會來攻擊他們。但唐吉訶德為他們的苦難感到自豪，他還常提醒桑丘，「艱苦的人生，會造就一顆堅毅的心」。

　　就在第四天太陽西下時，他們偶遇一群獵人，其中有一位身穿綠色絲絨的女子，她騎著一匹雄糾糾的白色種馬，手上還停著一隻獵鷹。

　　唐吉訶德驚訝地說：「女獵人，搞不好她還是一位公主。她一定想認識我。」

　　「她很有可能只想叫我們少管閒事。」桑丘笑著回答。

　　唐吉訶德對扈從的回答視若無睹，他命令桑丘說：「快點騎過去，向公主介紹我的來歷。」

　　桑丘嘴巴碎念著，鞭策驢子，往那一群人的方向騎去。

　　他說道：「親愛的女士，我的主人『霸獅騎士』，曾以『愁眉苦臉的騎士』為名，希望能……」

p. 90–91 女子打斷了他的話:「等等,你是說『愁眉苦臉的騎士』?」

「是的,我是他的扈從,桑丘……」

「潘薩?」女子笑著再度打斷他的話。

「是的,你認識我們嗎?」桑丘感到非常驚訝。

她答道:「當然囉,我讀過你們的冒險故事,那是我和我先生最喜愛的書了!」

「那我可以把他帶過來這裡嗎?」桑丘問道。

「請務必把他帶過來。」女子說。「你和你的主人一定要蒞臨我們位於附近的城堡,做我公爵丈夫的貴賓。」

當桑丘接受邀請時,公爵夫人暗自竊喜。事實上,她和她的丈夫都認為《唐吉訶德》是世上絕無僅有的諧劇。他們倆都是愛說笑話的人,她算計著說不定能拿這個瘋狂的騎士和他愚笨的助手來尋開心。

唐吉訶德和桑丘等一行人越過吊橋,發現自己置身於富麗的大城堡。兩位喇叭手吹奏樂器,迎接騎士的到來,唐吉訶德和桑丘身旁圍繞著一群散發出陣陣香氣的女僕。

p. 92–93 當天晚上,騎士和扈從與東道主相談甚歡,並享用了此生最豐富的佳餚。

公爵和公爵夫人興致高昂地聽著他們最近的冒險事蹟,不過他們最感興趣的,是有關杜爾西內雅的消息。

當他們提及杜爾西內雅,騎士難過地答道:「我最美麗的杜爾西內雅小姐,被邪惡的巫師變成一個騎著驢子的粗俗婦人了。」

「實在是太可怕了!」公爵夫人憋笑著說,她快忍俊不禁了。

隔天，公爵和公爵夫人說服唐吉訶德和他們一同前往森林狩獵野豬，但實際上他們密謀了一個計畫，要來狠狠地捉弄騎士和他的扈從。

　　當他們進行狩獵時，森林內突然傳來一陣噪音。

　　「一定是我的手下捉到野豬了。快跟我們一起來，小心地的長牙！」公爵夫人說道。

　　但當他們前去一探究竟時，發現半隻野豬都沒有。反之，卻看見一頭黑色的種馬在面前飛躍，上頭坐著一位身覆枝葉及長春藤的男子。

p. 94–95 「我是森林裡的精靈！」這個戴著綠色面具、頭帶牛角的怪人大叫：「森林中的魔鬼命我傳達一個訊息給遊俠騎士——唐吉訶德·拉曼查！」

　　「我就是唐吉訶德。」騎士答道。

　　「去破除你那美麗的杜爾西內雅的魔咒吧！」精靈繼續說道：「你必須要做兩件事：第一，你的扈從必須鞭打他自己。」

　　「要鞭打幾次？」桑丘尖叫問道。

　　「三千三百次。」

　　桑丘嚇到整個人都傻住了。

　　「不過首先，你必須騎著一匹飛馬越過山區，這匹馬正在公爵的城堡裡等著你。如果你真的具備足夠的勇氣，順利完成這兩項任務，你的摯愛杜爾西內雅就會從魔咒中脫困。」森林精靈說道。

精靈在説完話後轉身騎走。

「這是個奇蹟！」公爵夫人大叫：「我們要立刻返回城堡！」

「沒錯，不過首先，桑丘，先把我的鞭子拿來。」唐吉訶德大喊：「我們騎馬時，你可以開始鞭打你自己！」

這個驚嚇過度的扈從，已經騎著馬溜走，遠離騎士的控制。

p. 96–97 故事的場景回到城堡內。每個僕人都忙得團團轉，塔樓裡傳來驚恐的叫聲。庭院的中央有一隻巨大的木馬。僕人告訴公爵，木馬突然神奇地從天而降。就在此時，唐吉訶德正和桑丘爭論著，身為扈從的他必須忍受鞭打，才得以拯救杜爾西內雅的事情。

「我才不會做這種傻事。」桑丘大喊。

「為了我親愛的杜爾西內雅，我求你了。」唐吉訶德抽噎著説。

公爵夫人來到他們旁邊。「你們兩個停止無謂的爭吵吧。」她説道，並帶他們前往庭院。她時時刻刻都非常享受這個與丈夫共謀出來的天大惡作劇。

唐吉訶德目瞪口呆地看著那隻木馬。

「好驚人的動物啊！牠一定有二十英尺高！」

桑丘因恐懼而感到雙腳發軟。木馬的一邊有繩梯可以讓他們攀爬上去。公爵和公爵夫人看他們兩個人騎上木馬的樣子，簡直笑不可抑。

當他們坐上馬時，桑丘卻發現無處可扶，便用雙手抓住唐吉訶德褲子的腰帶。

p. 98–99 「這裡的木頭刻了字！」唐吉訶德大聲說道：「上面說，如果不矇眼駕馭這匹神馬，就必死無疑！」

「我有一條手帕！」桑丘說。

他拿出手帕、撕成兩半，把其中一半給他的主人。這兩個人將半邊的臭手帕綁在臉上，陽台上的公爵和公爵夫人則笑呵呵地看著這兩個騎在木馬上的蠢蛋。

騎士和扈從一矇上眼，一位僕人輕拍木馬，木馬裡面的僕人就將木馬往上抬了三英尺高，並且來回地劇烈搖晃。

「我們到達雲端了，桑丘。」唐吉訶德大叫。

「我好暈。」桑丘嗚咽。

騎士和扈從的對面陽台上有四位女僕，她們為風箱打氣，並潑入一杯杯的水。

「抓緊了，桑丘，我們正飛入一個暴風雨！」唐吉訶德大喊。

p. 100–101 看到此景的公爵和公爵夫人笑得欲罷不能，不過他們也因為戲弄這樣一個好騎士，而開始感到內疚。公爵示意男管家，要進行偉大的收尾了。

此時一位僕人點燃木馬的尾巴，裡頭藏著的上百個煙火瞬間引爆，發出了「砰」和「霹啪」的爆炸聲。桑丘緊緊抱住騎士，嚎啕大哭地說：「主人，救我，我答應接受鞭刑了！」

「一下都不少？」唐吉訶德問道。

「一下都不少！」桑丘答道。

接著唐吉訶德用拳頭打了木馬的頂端，不過這舉動只導致木馬裡頭的僕人晃動得更厲害。最後，由於僕人使馬身過於傾斜，整隻木馬就跌撞到了地面上。桑丘和騎士被拋向遠方，

安全地降落在城堡草坪的柔軟草地上。這些僕人趕緊將木馬搬到別的地方。

就在唐吉訶德和桑丘扯掉眼睛上矇著的碎布時，他們看到公爵夫人靠在他們身邊，表現出一副很關心他們的樣子。

「歡迎回來，」她溫柔地說著：「你們已經消失好幾個小時了。我們都很擔心！發生什麼事了？」

p. 102–103 桑丘和唐吉訶德休息了幾天，接著騎士向大家宣告，該是告別的時候了。

「那桑丘的鞭刑呢？」公爵夫人問道。她可不想錯過這精彩的一幕。

「在我們接下來的旅途上，他會完成所有的鞭刑。在宮廷的這些日子，讓我的右臂變軟弱了。是時候該走了，謝謝你們殷勤的款待。」

唐吉訶德和桑丘・潘薩往海邊騎去，前往巴塞隆納城市。

隔天早上，唐吉訶德告訴桑丘：「我現在要親眼看著你完成部分的鞭刑。」

桑丘一躍而起大聲說：「不要逼我，而且，我想要私下完成鞭刑。」

「我不管你要怎麼做，總之我要聽見每一下的鞭笞聲，這樣我才能確定你不是在敷衍我。」

桑丘不耐煩地說：「好，我現在就開始。」

他捉住繩子，踏著重重的腳步走到樹木前，接著解開衣服的鈕釦，用繩子重擊樹幹。

「噢！」他大叫：「這一下幾乎要見血了！」

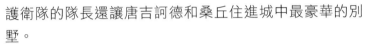

p. 104–105　幾天之後,當唐吉訶德和桑丘抵達巴塞隆納時,每個人都知道他們到來的消息。

　　街上聚集廣大的群眾,大家都想親眼目睹這位瘋狂卻高貴的騎士。人們對他們拋花,並予以歡呼,護衛隊的隊長還讓唐吉訶德和桑丘住進城中最豪華的別墅。

　　他們這幾個禮拜過著如帝王般的生活,每日接見將軍、海軍上將和政府的高級官員。

　　每天早上,唐吉訶德都會帶著羅西南多沿著海邊小跑。之後有一天,他在進行晨間小跑時,看見一個人沿著海灘向他靠近。那個人是一名戴著面甲且全副武裝的騎士。唐吉訶德向他靠近時,他可以看見騎士胸口的月形徽章。

　　「站住,『霸獅騎士』!」「白月騎士」叫住他:「我要向你挑戰。」

p. 106–107　「唐吉訶德隨時都準備接受挑戰。」這個西班牙老紳士無畏地回答。

　　「那麼我們來騎馬比武吧。」陌生的騎士說道,並舉起一把閃閃發亮的新長矛。

　　「說出你的條件吧。」唐吉訶德說。

　　「如果你贏了,這匹好馬和新的長矛將屬於你。但如果我贏了,你就必須退休,結束你的遊俠騎士生涯。」

　　「退休?」唐吉訶德大叫:「但這是不可能的。」

　　「我們這些年輕的騎士已經受夠你搶走了所有的風采,我們要你回到你的村子去安享晚年。」

　　「我接受你的條件!」唐吉訶德厲聲說道。

兩位騎士分別轉過身去檢查各自的武器。然而當他們轉回來時，説時遲那時快，「白月騎士」策馬猛然將長矛刺向唐吉訶德。

　　由於他無懈可擊的一擊，老騎士無從反抗，從馬鞍上摔了下去。他跌在滿是沙子的淺水海灘上，「白月騎士」隨即下馬，將劍壓在唐吉訶德的脖子上。

p. 108–109「你已經徹底失敗了，你服輸了嗎？」「白月騎士」問道。

　　「但這表示我的人生也玩完了，」唐吉訶德啜泣地説道：「沒了騎士精神，我就一無是處了。」

　　「你向我保證過的。」勝利者吼叫道。

　　「我會退隱江湖的，」唐吉訶德咳嗽地説道：「就如同我承諾的一般。」

　　騎士的眼淚交雜著鹽巴與海水。「這是我冒險中最黑暗的一天。」他感嘆地説。

　　「白月騎士」一點也不同情他，騎著坐騎就離開了。這個心碎的西班牙紳士跌坐在浪花裡，啜泣不已。

　　不久，唐吉訶德步履蹣跚地回到鎮上，他沒想到，「白月騎士」其實就是幾個月前被他擊敗的「森林騎士」，也就是年輕的卡拉斯科。「森林騎士」自從戰敗了，就不斷精進騎馬比武與馬術，下定決心要向唐吉訶德復仇，並送這位精神異常的西班牙紳士回家鄉。

　　當桑丘聽説唐吉訶德打輸了、準備退休，他感到非常難過。

「您不能放棄，主人。老狗學不了新把戲。」

「我對他承諾過。現在幫我脫下盔甲，我不再需要它了。」

在返回家鄉的三天路途上，這兩個人為自己的命運感到悲痛。

p. 110–111 一天晚上，這兩個男人在河邊紮營，桑丘整天想著要讓這個心碎的騎士打起精神。

「我要怎麼做，才會讓你心情好一點？」他問道。

「如果我知道親愛的杜爾西內雅安全無虞，那麼我應該會再次感到開心。」唐吉訶德說。

於是桑丘走到附近的樹林，每鞭打樹幹一下，就發出一聲慘叫聲。當桑丘把樹皮都鞭打下來時，唐吉訶德告訴他，一千次的鞭打已經完成，所以今天可以先停下來。

「我以你為榮，」唐吉訶德親切地告訴他：「如果你每晚都鞭打自己一千下，那等我們回到村子時，杜爾西內雅就自由了。」

他們艱苦地騎馬度過每一天，途經許多過往冒險的地方。每一晚，桑丘都會找一棵合適的樹來鞭打，並計算一千下。就在第四個早晨，他完成了最後的兩百四十八下。唐吉訶德握了桑丘的手，對他說，如果我們有下一次的冒險，我會多付你兩倍的薪水。

p. 112–113 當唐吉訶德回到自己家中的庭院時，女管家一看到他，驚訝地把手中的洗好的衣服給打翻在地上。

「主人，你安然無恙地回來了。」她哭著說。

「我現在很虛弱，」唐吉訶德輕聲地說道：「桑丘，扶我進房。」

這位西班牙老紳士一躺到床上，就昏睡了六天之久。他高燒不退，在沈睡中不斷地哭喊呻吟，彷彿是惡夢纏身。而他的朋友們同時耐心地在一旁守候著他。一個禮拜後，他睜開雙眼，看見站在床尾的牧師和理髮師。

「我回來了。」老騎士低聲嘀咕。

「唐吉訶德！」他們齊聲喊道，並衝到他的身旁。

「我的名字是阿隆索・吉哈納，」床上的男人說道：「我之前瘋了，但我現在已經清醒了。」

「真的嗎？騎士精神和巫師，這些東西都從你的腦袋裡消失得一乾二淨了嗎？」牧師問道。

「都消失了，」他溫和地答道：「我正常到連我自己快死了都曉得。」

p. 114-115 西班牙紳士病入膏肓的消息在村子裡傳得沸沸揚揚。桑丘從他工作的地方飛奔過來，現身於房中並跪在前主人的旁邊。

「你或許是有點瘋狂，」桑丘啜泣地說：「但如果你仍是騎士，就不應該死去。」

「你那個曾經是騎士的朋友，已經不在這裡了。」西班牙紳士回答：「你應該要忘了他。」

「我做不到。」扈從難過地說。

桑丘想去說服他的老朋友別放棄自己的靈魂，然而這個老西班牙紳士已經被高燒所打倒。桑丘在他的病榻前等了三天，最後老騎士還是離開了人世。

這就是唐吉訶德・拉曼查這個勇敢騎士的人生收尾。他的瘋狂行為，為他完成了常人只能想像的英勇事蹟。他的傳奇故事為後人傳誦了四百餘年。

　　安息吧，高貴的唐吉訶德。願你的探索是崇高的，願你的冒險為你帶來榮耀……

Answers

P. 30   **A**   **1** (c)   **2** (d)   **3** (a)   **4** (b)

         B   **1** chivalry   **2** hidalgo   **3** dub   **4** battle

P. 31   **C**   **1** (b)   **2** (a)

         D   **1** F   **2** T   **3** T   **4** F   **5** T

P. 48   **A**   **1** (c)   **2** (d)   **3** (b)   **4** (a)

         B   **1** (c)   **2** (a)   **3** (b)

P. 49   **C**   **1** (c)   **2** (a)

         D   **2** → **5** → **4** → **3** → **1**

P. 64   **A**   **1** (b)   **2** (c)   **3** (d)   **4** (a)

         B   **1** fled   **2** gushing   **3** lunatic   **4** feast   **5** greet

P. 65   **C**   **1** (c)   **2** (b)

         D   **1** T   **2** F   **3** T   **4** F

P. 84   **A**   **1** (c)   **2** (b)   **3** (a)   **4** (d)

         B   **1** (a)   **2** (b)   **3** (b)

P. 85   **C**   **1** (b)   **2** (c)

         D   **3** → **4** → **1** → **5** → **2**

P. 116　**A**　**1** (c)　**2** (a)　**3** (d)　**4** (b)

　　　　B　**1** (a)　**2** (c)　**3** (b)

P. 117　**C**　**1** (c)　**2** (b)

　　　　D　**1** F　**2** T　**3** F　**4** T　**4** T

P. 132　**A**　**1** He studied jousting and horsemanship so he could have revenge on Don Quixote. (Carrasco)
　　　　　　2 He was an old hidalgo who loved adventure stories. (Don Quixote)
　　　　　　3 He was a fat farmer who was very stupid. (Sancho Panza)
　　　　　　4 They pretended to believe Don Quixote so they could play jokes on him. (the Duke and Duchess)

　　　　B　**1** What was a hidalgo? (b)
　　　　　　2 What did Don Quixote think the barber's basin that he wore on his head was? (c)

P. 133　**C**　**1** code, chivalry　**2** regained, sanity
　　　　　　3 smashed, chest　**4** groaned, spurred
　　　　　　5 handkerchief, tore

　　　　D　**1** Don Quixote thought an evil wizard often robbed him of his glory. (T)
　　　　　　2 Don Quixote bravely guarded a magic trough. (T)
　　　　　　3 Don Quixote loved to eat, drink, and sleep more than anything else on earth. (F)
　　　　　　4 Sancho Panza was a courageous knight-errant. (F)
　　　　　　5 Don Quixote was killed by a hungry lion. (F)

唐吉訶德【二版】
Don Quixote

作者 _ 塞萬提斯
　　　（Miguel de Cervantes Saavedra）
改寫 _ Michael Robert Bradie
插圖 _ Nika Tchaikovskaya
翻譯 _ 歐寶妮
編輯 _ 賴祖兒 / 歐寶妮
作者 / 故事簡介翻譯 _ 王采翎
校對 _ 陳慧莉
封面設計 _ 林書玉
排版 _ 葳豐 / 林書玉
製程管理 _ 洪巧玲
發行人 _ 周均亮
出版者 _ 寂天文化事業股份有限公司
電話 _ +886-2-2365-9739
傳真 _ +886-2-2365-9835
網址 _ www.icosmos.com.tw
讀者服務 _ onlineservice@icosmos.com.tw
出版日期 _ 2020年11月 二版一刷（250201）
郵撥帳號 _ 1998620-0 寂天文化事業股份有限公司

Adaptor of *"Don Quixote"*

Michael Robert Bradie

Auburn University (BA - Communications)
a freelance writer

國家圖書館出版品預行編目資料

唐吉訶德 /Miguel de Cervantes Saavedra 原著；
Michael Robert Bradie 改寫 . -- 二版 . -- [臺北市] :
寂天文化, 2020.11
　　面；　公分
譯自 : Don Quixote.
ISBN 978-986-318-948-0(平裝附光碟片)

1. 英語 2. 讀本
805.18　　　　　　　　　　109016539